BRIGHEST MORNING DEW

Blessing Amu

Auc**J**us Publishers

Auctuspublishers.com

Published by Auctus Publishers

606 Merion Avenue, First Floor Havertown, PA 19083

Printed in the United States of America

ISBN (Print): 979-8-9915910=2-7

ISBN (Electronic): 979-8-9915910-3-4

Library of Congress Control Number: 2024947627

To EVERYONE who recognized my creative writing skills and encouraged me to get this inspiring novella to YOU!

Contents

CHAPTER ONE

THE JOHNSON FAMILY

The Johnson family was renowned for its esteemed reputation. Mr. Ernest Johnson, the head of the family of five, was a distinguished lawyer who gained widespread recognition for his involvement in the landmark election petition hearing at the Supreme Court. The case revolved around alleged irregularities and election rigging, prompting the opposition party to seek legal redress. Mr. Johnson's law firm was hired, and he served as the lead counsel for the petitioners. Renowned for his eloquence and exceptional ability to derive logical conclusions from limited information, he persuasively argued the case, influencing the jury's decision to order a rerun of the elections. Consequently, the opposition party emerged victorious in the subsequent general election, propelling Mr. Johnson to nationwide prominence.

Mrs. Cynthia Johnson, a woman of remarkable beauty and sophistication, aged approximately forty-six, held the position of deputy director at the Ghana Cocoa Board. Renowned for her diligent work ethic and strict adherence to punctuality, she hailed from the Volta Region of Ghana, whereas her husband, Mr. Johnson, traced his roots to the Central Region. Ghana, a nation celebrated for its beauty and tranquility, has a high incidence of inter-tribal marriages. It is common for individuals to have ancestral ties to different regions and tribes, as exemplified by the scenario where one's grandmother may belong to the Dagomba tribe in the north, the grandfather to the Ashanti tribe in the south, while the individual identifies as Ga from the coastal areas due to their mother's marriage to a Ga man. Similarly, Mrs. Cynthia Johnson embodied this cultural blend, with her maternal lineage stemming from the Ashanti tribe and her paternal roots from the Ewe tribe.

Mrs. Cynthia Johnson had three children with Mr. Johnson. Their eldest, Frank Johnson, 23, worked as a human resource manager at the Tema Oil Refinery. He was concurrently pursuing a part-time master's degree in public administration at the University of Ghana. Frank was characterized by his introverted personality and a deep fascination with quantum physics.

Suzzy Esi Johnson, the second child, was a freshman at Cape Coast University in the Central Region of Ghana, studying accounting and finance. She possessed a remarkable gift of eloquence, earning her nickname "parrot of ancient wisdom" from Mrs. Johnson. Suzzy had a penchant for engaging in lengthy discussions on a wide range, leading many to believe she would excel in law or media. At 20 years old, Suzzy was a stunning beauty, boasting radiant ebony skin, a statuesque figure, and a captivating physique.

Suzzy, displayed remarkable academic prowess with an outstanding CGPA that consistently impressed. Her father took immense pride in her accomplishments and recognized her exceptional intelligence and analytical skills. Despite her success in accounting, her father harbored a wish that she had pursued law, considering her aptitude for critical thinking and questioning.

The youngest sibling, Erica Mawu Johnson, preferred to go by Mawu Johnson, eschewing her given first name. At 14 years old and in sixth grade, Mawu radiated infectious joy, always wearing a bright smile. Her father affectionately referred to her as the family's outlier due to her unconventional academic path, which diverged sharply from her siblings' achievements. Mawu had faced significant challenges in her academic journey, having changed schools four times due to relentless teasing from classmates about her struggles. Unlike her siblings, Mawu showed a keen interest in entertainment over academics, a trait that set her apart within the family.

Mawu was an ardent music enthusiast, harboring aspirations of becoming a professional musician in the future. She was always adorned with her headphones, engrossed in melodic tunes. Her headphones were a constant companion, never leaving her side, even during school hours, when she would discreetly indulge in musical interludes during breaks.

In a classroom setting, the teacher had not yet arrived. Mawu danced gracefully and sang melodiously in front of her peers, receiving enthusiastic applause. At the tender age of fourteen, she displayed remarkable talent, captivating everyone with her enchanting voice. Mawu had already established herself as a shining star within her school community, where her performances garnered widespread admiration. Her vocal prowess had a captivating quality that evoked deep emotions, bringing tears of joy to those who heard her. Mawu was, indeed, an incredibly talented musician.

Miss Lovia walked into the classroom, where Mawu was singing and dancing, oblivious to the teacher's presence. The room fell into a hush as Mawu continued her performance, but Miss Lovia's raised voice cut through the air, prompting Mawu to quickly take her seat.

"You don't know anything, yet you always want to fool in class. Stupid girl! Try this next time and I will walk you out of my class." Miss Lovia was visibly perturbed by Mawu's behavior.

Miss Lovia was in her mid-twenties, an incredibly beautiful, slim, light-skinned lady who stood at about five feet seven inches tall. She had a naturally curvaceous figure, well-endowed backside that swayed uncontrollably whenever she walked. All the male tutors couldn't help but notice her, and many wished to date her, but most lacked the confidence to approach her; the few who did muster the courage were ultimately rejected.

"I trust you are all aware that we have a class test for today.,"

"Yes, Madam," the class responded.

"Okay, everyone! Bring your bags over here and let's get started," she said, pointing to a corner. She distributed the test papers to them, and then they began.

"No copying please!" she cautioned.

Mawu sat frozen in her English class test, clueless about where to begin. She hadn't studied enough, and now she was paying the price. Sweat trickled down her forehead as she anxiously chewed on her pen. Miss Lovia noticed Mawu's distress, even in the chill of the air-conditioned room. Desperate for help, Mawu scanned the room, hoping someone would catch her eye, but her classmates were all too focused on their own tests.

"Mawu, are you alright?" Inquired Miss Lovia.

"Yes Madam," Mawu responded with a disingenuous smile.

Determined not to submit a blank answer sheet, Mawu carefully transcribed the comprehension story onto her paper. When it came to the Questions and Answers section, she adopted a more playfully approach, answering with a mix of randomness and excitement, as if she were participating in a lottery.

"Stop work! All pens on the table. Hands up." Miss Lovia gathered the test papers on their desks.

The bell chimed for break. Precious approached Mawu's desk. Among all the young ladies in the classroom, Mawu found solace in Precious, who was six months her senior. As the eldest students in the class, Precious and Mawu had a unique bond. However, their educational journeys had differed; Mawu had repeated a grade twice in different stages. While Precious exhibited remarkable fluency in the English language, Mawu meticulously crafted her words in her mind before articulating them.

"How did you find the test?" Inquired Precious.

"I did my best," Mawu replied.

They left the classroom and headed towards the school canteen, discussing the recent class test. Precious stood out as one of the most intellectually gifted students in the class, renowned for her exceptional aptitude for learning. She received admiration from all educators for her sharp intellect, with integrated Science and Mathematics being her two most proficient subjects.

"For Section B, I was totally stumped - I had no idea what to write!," Mawu admitted.

"But I saw you scribbling away like crazy! You looked so focused."

"Precious, I have to confess... I was basically just transcribing the comprehension essay onto my answer sheet. I had no idea what else to do!"

"No way! You're not serious, right?" Precious asked, her voice laced with surprise.

The cafeteria was abuzz with activity as students gathered to purchase their meals. A diverse range of culinary options was available for selection. Two quaint snack bars, located adjacent to the main dining area, offered an assortment of delectable treats. Golden Star International School was a premier educational institution in Accra, renowned for catering to the children of esteemed members of society. This earned it the nickname "School of Dada Bees" among the public.

"No way, the right answer for number nine is definitely 'AGAINST'!", stated one young lady.

Mawu turned and saw her peers engaged in a lively discussion about the examination they had just completed, so she decided to join them.

"Are you sure about that?" another young lady asked.

"What did you put for that question?" the first young lady asked, still thinking about the one where you had to choose an antonym for "FOR". "I'm sure it's 'AGAINST'," she said confidently.

The other girl's cheerful expression faltered, revealing she had mistakenly circled the wrong answer. Mawu couldn't remember which option she had chosen, having selected it on a whim. Her friends continued discussing until she finally joined in.

"Honestly, I was so confused! I thought 'LAUGH' was a synonym for 'SMILE', but it wasn't even an option. So, I just went with 'EXCITED'." The third girl replied to the second girl's question.

"I chose 'BEAM'," the first lady said.

"Beam? Like, a beam of light?" Mawu asked, sounding confused.

"A beam of shadows? That's a good one!" the young lady said, chuckling sarcastically.

They laughed...

"Looks like Rebecca's going to be the one carrying this class!" the young lady joked.

"God forbid! I can't be the one with bad grades, not when Mawu, the queen of subpar grades, is right here!"

They burst out laughing while taunting and ridiculing Mawu.

Mawu's history of changing schools was partly due to experiences like this. During academic discussions, her peers would incessantly taunt her. Precious, observing the scene, put down her meal and intervened, escorting Mawu away from the conflict.

CHAPTER TWO

UNEXPECTED FRIENDSHIP

It was a splendid Saturday morning at the fitness center, where individuals of both genders were engaged in their workouts. Among the four gyms nearby, Virgo Gym stood out for its state-of-the-art gymnastics' equipment. The vibrant sounds of Afrobeat music filled the air, setting the tempo for the exercises being performed. Mawu was focused on her muscle training, diligently lifting a dumbbell. With each repetition, her breathing quickened, indicating the intensity of her workout. Suddenly, she paused, taking a moment to reflect on how her father's disapproval had cast a shadow over her aspirations, despite her passion for pursuing a career in music. Closing her eyes briefly, tears welled up and trickled down her cheeks. Overcome with emotion, she allowed herself a few minutes to express her feelings before releasing a deep sigh of relief. Gently wiping away the tears with a pristine white towel draped around her neck, she was startled by a familiar male voice behind her.

"Hey, are those tears of joy or just a breakdown?" Ansah asked with a soft smile. "I didn't know goddesses like you were allowed to cry!"

"Wait a minute, do I know you from somewhere? Oh yeah, weren't you at the social park? Wait, are you following me or something?"

"Ha! Me, stalk you? No way! This is a public place, not your bedroom... unless you're stalking me, that is!" Ansah said with a warm grin.

"You don't mean it, let me pretend I didn't hear you say that."

"I had you pegged as this strong, confident woman after our conversation at the social park. But now, I'm shocked - I didn't think you were the emotional type!" Ansah teased.

"Tears don't mean you're weak, they mean you're strong enough to feel and keep going. It's a sign of resilience, not fragility."

"Wow, I didn't know you were a motivational speaker too! But seriously, I can tell you're going through some tough times. Your eyes say a lot. Would you be open to talking about it? By the way, I'm Ansah - we didn't get a chance to properly introduce ourselves the other day."

Mawu and Ansah strolled out of the fitness center and settled on a solid bench nestled beneath a flourishing tree just outside the gym. Ansah, sixteen years old, stood at 5 feet 8 inches with a dusky complexion and an athletic build. He was strikingly handsome, with a jovial demeanor that was accentuated by his dimple, which appeared whenever he flashed a warm smile.

"Have you ever felt pressured to give up on your own dreams and pursue a career path that your parents want for you, instead of what you truly want?"

"Well, no!"

"How do you handle it when your parents are pushing you to do something that you're really not passionate about? Do you speak up and tell them how you feel, or do you just nod and smile?"

"You know, the Bible says in Ephesians 6:1-3 that we should obey our parents because it's what God wants us to do. And when we honor them, it's like opening ourselves up to a blessing - we're promised a good life and a long one! Our parents have been around the block a few times, so they've got wisdom and insight to share. That's why it makes sense to listen to them and trust their guidance."

"Thanks so much for sharing your thoughts! I'm blown away by your knowledge of Bible verses - you're like a walking encyclopedia! But seriously, are you a Sunday school teacher or something? You're so knowledgeable! Anyway, it was great chatting with you, but I should probably get going. Take care."

"You're most welcome. I am so passionate about the bible, and I am not a Sunday school teacher but actually a pastor's son. However, I am still curious to know your name."

"My name is Mawu."

"Mawu? Don't you have any Christian name, I thought you are a Christian?"

"Yes, I am, but you're also Ansah. I thought you are also a Christian, yet you mentioned Ansah to me and not your Christian name either."

"I am Derrick Ansah. Derrick is my Christian name," he said warmly.

"Come on, where's Derrick even mentioned in the scriptures? It's a straight-up English name! You're looking more Western than Christian, if you ask me," Mawu teased.

"Well, at least I bear the name of those who brought us Christianity," he smiled.

"I'm super proud of my name and where it comes from! My ancestors were total heroes, defending our land and keeping our heritage alive. Their legacy lives on through me, and I'm all about embracing my Ewe and Fante roots from Keta and Saltpond. Oh, and my name? It's Mawufemo Afi Johnson, but call me Mawu - named after my amazing 'Mamaga' Mawufemo Ajo!" .

"Wow, so, you're a mix of two amazing ancestral lines - Voltarian and Fante! That's so cool, like two powerful bloodlines coming together in one person! Hey, Mama Africa, nice to meet you too! I'm stoked I could make you smile, that's totally awesome!"

"Thank you and bye."

Mawu was serious about her cultural heritage. When she started formal education as a child, her father added Erica to her name, but she later asked her parents to remove it, feeling it disconnected her from her roots. She preferred being called Mawufemo, for her name held spiritual significance in her native language, meaning "God's way." This reflected her approach to life, guided by her inner self. Each morning, Mawu meditated peacefully in her room before starting her day. Although raised Christian, she leaned towards spirituality over religiosity. Her actions were driven by her soul's desires, not external influences. Embracing her natural and indigenous roots, she chose traditional foods like "Akplè and green soup" over noodles. Her love for her mother tongue was evident, as she always preferred speaking her indigenous dialect over foreign languages, which led some peers to consider her provincial.

CHAPTER THREE

RESPONSIBLE FATHER, RATIONAL DAUGHTER

Mrs. Johnson was displeased with the way her husband had spoken to Mawu earlier. She believed that parents should never speak to their child or correct them disrespectfully, regardless of the child's misbehavior. Mrs. Johnson gently opened the bedroom door, entered gracefully, and approached Mr. Johnson calmly. He was reclining on the bed, his face hidden behind a book.

"You should have found a nicer way to talk to her," Mrs. Johnson admonished her husband. "She is hurt by the way you talked to her."

"You're spoiling her too much," Mr. Johnson remarked. "She needs to know that education is a big deal, and it's our job as parents to make sure she gets that."

The family was discussing the afternoon's events. They usually went to the mall every Saturday to watch movie, but that day, there was an unusual silence about it. During lunch, Mawu asked her mother if they would still go to the cinema as usual. However, Mr. Johnson sternly told Mawu to be quiet and focus on her food, implying that her interests were only about entertainment, not academics. His words, laced with exasperation, made Mawu stop eating abruptly and run to her room in tears. Mrs. Johnson disagreed with her husband's approach, but she chose to keep her thoughts to herself until they were alone in their bedroom.

"That doesn't mean you have to be harsh with her."

"Time for her to sit up straight! She's always got those headphones on, listening to who-knows-what. I'm thinking of taking them away so she can actually focus on her books for once." Mr. Johnson exited the bedroom.

Mr. Johnson had hoped that Mawu would follow in his footsteps and pursue a career in law, but she remained determined to forge her own path. He worried that without proper guidance, her ambitions might falter. Her underwhelming academic performance weighed heavily on his mind, causing him distress. He struggled to understand how a child of his, a man with scholarly achievements, could struggle academically. As he made his way downstairs, he ran into Mawu in the corridor.

"I've been getting complaints about your grades, and I'm not happy. We're a family that values education, so why are you slacking off? You need to step up your game! And another thing, no more music. That means no headphones, no singing along, nothing. You need to focus on your studies, not your playlists. Understand?" Mr. Johnson took the headset from Mawu's neck.

Mrs. Johnson stepped out of the bedroom and into the corridor, watching quietly. Mr. Johnson shifted his focus to her…

"Cynthia, you better talk to your daughter or else..."

"Our daughter, she has your DNA," Mrs. Johnson asserted firmly.

"Does she have my smarts too? I don't even want to think about it," Mr. Johnson said, his anger rising.

He stormed past Mrs. Johnson, his anger simmering, and went straight to his bedroom. Mawu's eyes welled up with tears, on the verge of streaming down her face. Overcome with sadness, she slipped quietly out of the corridor.

Mrs. Johnson thought aloud. "Anger can lead to hurtful words, and those words can leave lasting scars. Even after we've cooled off, the pain we caused can still linger. Think of it like a broken plate - once it's shattered, it's gone for good."

She swiftly made her way into the bedroom to confront her husband.

"What was the meaning of what you said over there?"

"The meaning of what I said is to tell your daughter to be serious with her books."

"Why do men often act like this when their kids don't live up to their expectations? When their kid does well, they're all about taking credit and bragging about it. But when their kid struggles, they suddenly act like the kid is only the mom's responsibility, even though they're the ones who helped create them in the first place!," she reflected awhile.

"You're talking about Mawu like she's not even your own child. Do you remember those late nights when we were intimate, and you were whispering sweet nothings in my ear, caressing me with passion? Now, you're spewing this hurtful nonsense just because she's not book-smart like us? How do you think she feels when you say those things in front of her?"

"Are you serious? You're going to blame me for wanting some affection? You're the one who got her that headset, which is probably distracting her from her schoolwork. Maybe you should take some responsibility for that."

"So, must you say she is not your daughter? Excuse me," Mrs. Johnson exited and banged the door shut.

Mawu sat in a swaying chair in the garden, tears cascading down her cheeks. Her father's harsh words and tone had deeply hurt her. Questions swirled in her mind: Was she truly Mr. Johnson's biological child? If not, who was her father? And if so, why was she being treated like an adopted child? These thoughts haunted her. It wasn't the fear of losing her parents or changing schools that worried her, but the dread that her musical journey might be suddenly stopped. Music was her passion, her reason for being; without it, her very existence would lose its meaning. Music was the foundation of her happiness, intricately woven into every aspect of her life.

Frank, her brother, gently caressed Mawu's back, prompting her to turn and meet his gaze. Seeing her tears, he offered his handkerchief to her. With a tender smile, he affectionately called her his "shining star."

"Hey, don't cry, little star! Everything will be okay. Don't take Daddy's words to heart, he doesn't mean to hurt you. He's just stressed out, that's all.."

"So, you know he hates me?"

"No, he doesn't. Not at all, he only wants the best for you."

"Frank, honestly, I'm just not feeling the whole classroom thing. My heart's really in music. I've been checking out this awesome music school in Adabraka and I'm totally stocked about it. Can you please help me convince Mom and Dad to let me enroll there? I know they're going to be worried about me giving up on academics, but I really feel this is what I'm meant to do."

Frank sat in a wicker chair that sat beside Mawu.

"I saw this awesome video today and it really made me think…" He looked into Mawu's eyes. "It said that water and steam are basically the same, just vibrating at different frequencies. And it got me thinking, if our emotions can shape our reality, then maybe our reality can also shape our emotions. It's like that whole thing about mass and energy being interchangeable - it's all about transformation."

"What you're looking for is also looking for you. Think of your thoughts like waves that send out energy and vibes. Just like how things can be solid and still have energy, our thoughts can be like waves that go beyond space and time. So, when you imagine what you want, you're basically saying it already exists in a different realm, like a parallel universe. It's not physical, but it's still out there in the form of energy."

"The quantum world is full of different realities, and our minds can tap into them. Everything is made of energy - our tears, thoughts, and emotions - all vibrating at different frequencies. Our thoughts create waves that shape our reality, powered by how we feel. To shift into the life we want, we need to match our vibe with our dreams, and our subconscious mind can help us do that."

"Controlling your emotions and thoughts is key. By changing the patterns in your subconscious, you can change your vibe. Your subconscious mind has a big impact on your thoughts, so it's important to focus on the good stuff and avoid dwelling on the bad. Most of the time, we think about the same old things we've always thought about, so we need to make an effort to think about what we want, not what we don't want. Take control of your thoughts and emotions, and don't let negative ones become a reality."

Mawu sat in contemplative silence, absorbing every word Frank said, before delicately clearing her throat.

"So, if my emotions and thoughts are all just energy, and even my tears are energy too... does that mean I'm vibrating at a frequency that's not really working for me?"

"Hey, I know you won't get everything right now, but trust me, a day will come when you'll go after your dreams with confidence. Your future is in your own hands! I'm your biggest cheerleader, don't forget that. And I'll be here supporting you every step of the way, for as long as I can."

"Frank, why are you speaking like someone who is going to die tomorrow?"

They both chuckled heartily.

"Go to my room, there's a headset on my bed, take it and use it but make sure nobody sees you with it."

Mawu happily jumped down and hurried to Frank's room.

The next day, Mrs. Johnson was in the kitchen preparing breakfast. She meticulously chopped the onions, tomatoes, spring onions, carrot, and green pepper. After filling the kettle with water, she turned it on and delicately cracked two eggs into a small bowl. Mixing in the finely chopped vegetables, she stirred the mixture with finesse. She drizzled a small amount of oil into a frying pan, then poured in the egg and vegetable mixture. Meanwhile, she sliced the bread into portions. Once the eggs were cooked to perfection, she skillfully assembled them in the bread and toasted it to a golden brown. She poured steaming water from the kettle into a cup containing a Lipton tea bag added a splash of milk. Placing the toasted bread on a dainty plate, she elegantly arranged it on a serving tray and carried it into the living room. Upon entering, she saw Mawu kneeling on the floor while Mr. Johnson lounged on the couch.

"Mawu, why are you kneeling?"

"Daddy asked me to kneel down."

"Honey, why?" Mrs. Johnson asked her husband.

"I walked in on her watching a music video, even though I've told her before not to listen to that kind of stuff at home or anywhere else.

"Let her get up and eat, she's not feeling great this morning. I turned on the TV and told her to stay here while I make her some food before she takes her meds."

He gestured for Mawu to rise, but instead, he rose and elegantly made his way through the exit door.

Chapter Four

FRANK'S PAINFUL DEMISE

Years later, when Mawu turned eighteen and graduated from senior high school, a new chapter of life began to unfold. As she navigated the world, she experienced the fullness of life firsthand. Although her WASCE results disappointing, with four consecutive "F's," that visibly displeased her father, Mawu remained unfazed by her academic setbacks. She stayed focused on her musical aspirations, pursuing them with unwavering dedication.

Frank was awarded a prestigious scholarship by his company to undertake a six-month program in the United States, aimed at preparing him to assume the role of Managing Director. This news brought immense joy to the Johnson family, prompting a celebratory party to honor Frank's promotion and success. With his departure for the States scheduled in three days, Mawu felt a mix of emotions. While she was thrilled for Frank's opportunity, she couldn't shake off the worry of missing a brother, a loyal friend, a mentor, and advisor. The looming question of who would offer her support during turbulent times in Frank's absence lingered in her mind.

Frank emerged from the living room and spotted Mawu sitting alone in the hallway. He grabbed a folder chair, set it beside her, and sat down. It was clear to Frank that Mawu was troubled; her demeanor radiated unease.

"Hey superstar, I won't be gone forever! It's just a six-month course. And don't worry, we'll talk every single day. You know something?"

Mawu shook her head to imply "no."

"I promise to buy you a beat machine when I'm coming back."

"Wow, are you serious?" Mawu was excited.

"Yes, but let's keep that a secret."

Mawu embraced Frank tightly, her eyes welling up with tears of joy as Frank gently patted her back.

"Hey, cheer up! I totally believe in you and your dreams. You're meant for great things. Just remember to always trust yourself and your vision, no matter what others say or what obstacles come up. Listen to your inner voice and stay in control of your thoughts. Don't let fear or doubt hold you back - you got this!"

****

The day Frank's departure to the States had finally arrived. The family accompanied him to the airport, where his flight was scheduled to depart at 2 pm in that afternoon. They arrived at 1 pm and waited until it was time to board. After bidding him farewell and wishing him safe travels, they watched as he departed. Frank's absence would be felt by all.

That same evening, Mr. Johnson was wheeled into a wards at the Korle-Bu Teaching Hospital on a stretcher, accompanied by two nurses, while Mrs. Johnson followed closely behind. Mr. Johnson's blood pressure had skyrocketed due to shock. After the nurse finished checking his vital signs, she started an intravenous drip to stabilize him. Meanwhile, Suzzy and Mawu rushed into the ward, having been filled in on the situation by Mrs. Johnson, who had called them after the incident occurred.

"Nurse, please, is our father, okay?" Suzzy's expression filled with concern.

"His pressure went up, but he will be fine. Excuse me please." the nurse exited the ward.

"Mom, what happened?" Mawu asked.

"The nurse said he will be fine." Mrs. Johnson was still shedding tears.

"I heard the nurse too, Mom, but what's really going on?" Mawu wasn't buying her mom's story and was suspicious of her tears.

Suzzy, noticing Mawu's persistent questioning of their mother, gestured for her to stop. Shortly after, Mr. Johnson regained consciousness, prompting Mrs. Johnson to send Mawu to call the nurse.

A couple of hours later, Mr. Johnson was discharged, and they arrived home safely. But Mawu sensed a veil of secrecy surrounding her parents, leaving her with a nagging feeling of unease that sparked an internal struggle.

"Dad, what's going on? The nurse said your blood pressure spiked because of a shock. Is everything okay?"

"Mawu, can't you just let your dad rest? We just got back from the hospital..." Mrs. Johnson's voice trailed off as she burst into tears.

Mr. Johnson tried to hold back tears, but his emotions eventually got the better of him. Meanwhile, Mawu and Suzzy's curiosity grew as they sensed their parents were hiding something.

"Daddy, is somebody dead?" Suzzy questioned.

Suzzy's question sent Mawu's heart sinking into her stomach, as a wave of fear gripped her. A surge of heat flushed through her body, causing sweat to break out on every pore. If the topic was indeed mortality, she desperately hoped it didn't involve her beloved brother and rock, Frank. Although she longed to ask her father about Frank's well-being, she hesitated, fearful of the answer. Before she could think of what to do next...

"Is Frank okay, daddy?" Suzzy asked.

Mr. and Mrs. Johnson's lamentations grew more intense after Suzzy's inquiry . Mawu's knees buckled, her vision blurred, her heart racing wildly, and a bitter taste filled her mouth. Meanwhile, Suzzy struggled to maintain her composure, overwhelmed by her parents' emotional outpouring and desperate for clarity.

"Will someone speak up now!" Suzzy screamed.

"Frank is no more, Frank is dead!" Mrs. Johnson cried.

Earlier that evening, Mr. Johnson was watching the news in the living room when a breaking report announced that a plane bound for the United States had crashed, resulting in no survivors among its passengers. Shockingly, Frank had been on that very flight. Mrs. Johnson caught the tail end of the broadcast before her husband collapsed and was rushed to the hospital.

The words "Frank is no more" reverberated in Mawu's mind, echoing from a distance, refusing to fade. She felt utterly disorientated, unable to hear anything else. Suzzy saw Mawu sink to the ground in a slow, cinematic motion. Suzzy's heart ached, and she too collapsed, overcome by dizziness. Their parents rushed to their aid. Mr. Johnson hastened to the kitchen, returned with a glass of water, and tenderly sprinkled droplets on their pale faces, slowly restoring their consciousness. As they came to, they were swiftly transported to the hospital.

Three months had passed since Frank's passing, a period marked by immense challenges for the Johnson family. Despite their struggles, they found solace in believing Frank was now at peace. However, Mawu grappled with the apparent injustice of God's actions, questioning why a kind-hearted brother like Frank had been taken while her antagonistic father, who had constantly undermined her dreams, remained.

Defying her parents' wishes, Mawu refused to attend remedial classes to boost her university admission prospects. She saw this endeavor as futile and wasteful, as her true passion lay in music and entertainment. Music wasn't just a hobby to Mawu; it was an integral part of her being, the essence of her existence. Nothing brought her the same profound joy and fulfillment as music did.

"Your dad is really upset with you for refusing to go to the remedial classes. Sweetie, please listen to us. We just want what's best for you. We want you to have an amazing future, one that we can all be proud of. Can't you just try to see things from your dad's perspective and do what he wants? Please?" Mrs. Johnson said.

"What do you mean 'what your father wants you to be'? Are you saying you're not on his side? That you don't agree with what he wants for me?"

"Your father and I are on the same page when it comes to what's best for you. We're in this together."

"Mom, I'm sorry, but I'm really done with school. I just can't do it anymore," Mawu said politely.

"Mawu, are you telling me you're done with your education? Just like that? You're willing to settle for barely scraping by with poor grades in senior high school? That's not acceptable! Our family has a reputation to uphold, and I won't let you tarnish it with your lack of ambition. Why are you so determined to disappoint us, to bring shame to our name?" Mrs. Johnson expressed her disappointment.

"Mom, those are Daddy's words, not yours. But what's wrong with being a musician? Why can't I pursue my passion for music? It's what makes me happy, and I'm good at it. Why can't that be enough?"

"A secular musician? Really? That's not a great choice. Our family has a certain image to maintain. If you wanted to do Christian music, maybe your dad would be cool with it. But look at your siblings - Frank was a boss at Tema Oil Refinery, and Suzzy is crushing it at Zenith Bank. And you want to be a musician? That's not exactly impressive. You need to think this through before you make a mistake you can't fix." Mrs. Johnson walked out, visibly displeased.

Mawu was astonished. Could this really be her mother? Besides Frank, who had always wholeheartedly supported her passion, her mother had been her most reliable admirer. However, her mother's harsh words and actions had caught her completely off guard. Now, she felt utterly isolated, with no one standing by her side. Determined to take control of her own destiny and stay true to the music within her, she vowed to persevere until she achieved her dream. She refused to abandon her own passion to satisfy her parents' desires.

Mrs. Johnson personally had no objections to Mawu's musical aspirations, but she chose to stand by her husband as the head of the household. To maintain harmony and respect his authority, she grew tired of the escalating disputes between her husband and daughter. As the sun set peacefully, she Joined her husband in the garden, finding him lost in the evening's tranquility, reading a newspaper.

"Sweetheart, please, can we talk?" Mrs. Johnson asked.

"What is it, honey?"

"Sweetheart, let's give Mawu the chance to chase her passion for music. Music school could be perfect for her. We can't assume everyone needs to be a lawyer or doctor. Think about all the successful people who didn't do great in school but excelled in their fields. Education comes in many forms. Can we rethink our approach on this?"

"My daughter is not going to be some rockstar gangster. Have you seen what those musicians wear? The way they live? No way am I letting her become one of them. Not happening under my roof."

"Look, there are lawyers who seem perfect on the outside - fancy suits, nice ties - but are actually corrupt to the core. Does that mean all lawyers are bad? Come on. And let's not forget, our daughter comes from a good family, raised with strong Christian values. I'm asking you to rethink this."

"She's been raised Christian, I get that. So, she should be singing gospel music, not that crazy music. Honestly, she's already embarrassing our family enough, let's not add that music mess to it.."

"How can you say that, Sweetheart? Just because she's not book-smart doesn't mean she's not talented. Mawu's always said music is her thing, so why can't you just get it and let her do her thing? It's her dream, for crying out loud!"

"Secular music is not welcome in my home, especially considering the company it keeps. If Mawu wants to indulge in that sort of thing, she's free to do so elsewhere, but not under my roof! And since she's 18 now, she's an adult and can make her own choices - just not in my house."

"Are you seriously suggesting Mawu should move out? Oh, sweetheart, that's extreme. You're really willing to push our daughter away over music?"

Suzzy's bedside alarm chimed, signaling the start of a new day - Saturday, to be precise. She had set the alarm the previous night to ensure she would wake up promptly at 6:00 a.m., allowing enough time to prepare for the office meeting scheduled to commence at 8:00 a.am. After bathing and dressing, Suzzy realized her belt was missing. Unwilling to waste precious time searching for it due to the expected weekend traffic, she decided to ask her sister, Mawu, for help. Upon entering Mawu's room, Suzzy was surprised to find it empty. She called out for Mawu, asking if she was in the adjacent bathroom, but received no response. Puzzled by her sister's absence at such an early hour, Suzzy tried to contact Mawu via phone, only to find it was switched off. Feeling a sense of unease, Suzzy rushed to her parents' bedroom and informed them of the situation.

Without delay, her mother joined Suzzy in searching Mawu's room. After thoroughly searching the entire lower level of the house, including the kitchen and living areas, Mawu was still nowhere to be found. Growing increasingly concerned for her sister's well-being, Mrs. Johnson directed Suzzy to call the security guard. Moments later, Suzzy returned with the security guard, who was holding a piece of paper.

"Please, Mawu asked me to give you this when you wake up," the security guard said, handing the envelope to Mrs. Johnson.

"Mom, I'm sorry, but Dad's right. I can't stay here and disagree with him all the time. I'm 18 now, so I need to take control of my own life. I'll come back home successful, but for now, please pray for me and bless me. Tell Suzzy I love her so much, and Mom, I love you more than anything. And Dad, even though we don't see eye to eye, I respect him deeply. Goodbye!" The letter read.

Overcome with sorrow, they all struggled to cope, even the security guard. Suzzy was distraught and had to notify the office that she would be unable to attend the meeting due to a pressing emergency requiring her immediate attention at home. Tears continued to stream down Mrs. Johnson's cheeks.

CHAPTER FIVE

SURVIVING THE GHETTO

Mawu emerged from a banger parked in one of the ghettos of the market. The soft morning light cast a warm glow over the surroundings as she carefully tore open the corner of the sachet water she held, using it to wash her face. After rinsing her mouth, she discarded the remaining water. Just then, Adjei's voice pierced the stillness, calling out her name.

"Mawu, we got a load."

Adjei was the one who offered Mawu a place to stay when she was wandering in the market. He had been a fixture in the market for five years, ever since his life was turned upside down by a tragedy. At thirteen, Adjei lost his mother in a fatal car accident, and his father showed little concern for his well-being. As only child, Adjei was left to fend for himself after his father abandoned their home to live with another woman in the same neighborhood where his mother had rented a place. With no family support, Adjei turned to the market for survival, finding refuge with a friend and working hard as a head porter. Despite his tough circumstances, Adjei's diligence and compassionate nature shone through in everything he did.

Mawu and Adjei, determined and hardworking individuals, began their daily routine in the bustling market, where they worked tirelessly as truck pushers. Their synchronized efforts were on full display as Adjei skillfully steered the front while Mawu exerted her strength at the back, creating a harmonious dance of labor and perseverance. Despite their unwavering dedication, life within the market walls proved to be a relentless challenge, testing their resilience. With only meager earnings, they could afford to eat just once a day, a sacrifice they made in pursuit of their ambitious dreams.

In the market realm, money held supreme power, determining the quality of life one could afford. Even basic necessities like using the restroom or maintaining personal hygiene came with a price, exposing the harsh reality of survival in such an environment. Women faced additional challenges, particularly during menstruation, suffering excruciating pain and discomfort while laboring under the unforgiving sun. Some were forced to resort to sex work as a means of survival, a heartbreaking consequence of societal neglect and economic inequality.

Despite the struggles and adversities, talents bloomed within the market's confines, yet were overshadowed by the pervasive influence of drugs and social decay. Dreams were shattered, and destinies altered by circumstances beyond their control. A vicious cycle of addiction and despair gripped many, leading them down a path they never intended to take. The poignant tales of individuals whose potential was stifled by a flawed system served as a stark reminder of the harsh realities faced by those marginalized in society.

One evening, Mawu was strolling through the alleys of the impoverished neighborhood when she stumbled upon a quaint establishment. The compact bar had a row of plastic chairs artfully arranged in front of it, inviting patrons to unwind. Disco lights were strategically placed inside and outside the bar for aesthetic appeal. Mawu observed young men and women engaging in illicit activities; one young man carefully mixed a powdery substance into a cup, swirling it to ensure proper mixing. As he consumed the concoction, its effects quickly took hold, manifesting in peculiar behavior and slowed actions. He eventually stood motionless, oblivious to his surroundings, joined by a small group of similarly affected young men. Mawu noticed a young woman of her age, carrying a child on her back, and wondered why she was there. This young lady had come to buy alcohol. Other young women were meticulously rolling marijuana into brown and white papers. Every activity within the bar revolved around illegal substances. Mawu was shocked to see two uniformed police officers seated among the drug users, casually indulging in marijuana. Undeterred, she sat in a nearby plastic chair and struck up a conversation with the young lady carrying the child.

"Hi, good evening," Mawu greeted.

"Fine girl, how be market?" The young woman mistook Mawu for a courtesan. "You wan buy me cigarette?"

"I don't smoke," Mawu said.

"Oh, holy Ashawo." The young woman was inebriated.

"I am sorry but I'm not a prostitute," Mawu said with a gentle smile.

The young woman's face lit up with a warm, radiant smile as she turned to Mawu once more.

"Who you dey lie for? So, who be you if you no be Ashawo?"

"My name is Mawu."

The baby whimpered softly, and the mother tenderly unwrapped her from her back, cradling her in her arms. With a gentle finger, she unbuttoned her blouse and nursed the baby, guiding her to latch on.

"Oh, so she is your baby?" Mawu asked.

"Yes, she is Lina."

"I think Lina's had enough of this loud music and just wants to head home and sleep, you know?, It's clearly overwhelming her," Mawu grinned.

"Yes, you're right." She was drifting into slumber when Mawu gently tapped her shoulder, rousing her . With a fluid motion, she secured Lina to her back once more but struggled to find her balance as she rose to her feet. Mawu's steady hand caught hers, offering a reassuring grip that prevented her from stumbling.

"Let me walk you home," Mawu offered.

"Thank you."

"I still don't know your name."

"My name is Mabel," she said.

Mawu walked alongside Mabel as she escorted her home, the moon casting a soft glow on the path ahead. With a gentle smile, Mawu mentioned that she would visit Mabel and her daughter Lina the following day, warming Mabel's heart with the gesture. Grateful for the company, Mabel thanked Mawu before they parted ways for the night.

As soon as Mawu arrived home, she eagerly sought out Adjei, bursting to share the evening's events with him. She recounted her time with Mabel and the bar, stressing the alarming rate at which young people were getting hooked on hard drugs. Adjei listened attentively, nodding thoughtfully as Mawu shared her concerns.

On Sunday morning, Mawu got ready and took Adjei with her to visit Mabel. When they arrived, Mabel was already up, tenderly bathing Lina in a basin of water. Mawu and Adjei exchanged warm greetings with her, and she responded graciously. Mabel studied their faces, trying to recall where she had met them before. Mawu's face seemed vaguely familiar, but she couldn't quite place it..

"Oh, I remember you! you're the one who walked me home last night! What's your name again?"

"Mawu"

"Yes, yes, yes... I remember now. Is he your brother?" Mabel alluded to Adjei.

"Yes, his name is Adjei. We all live in this ghetto," Mawu said.

"Oh charlie, you guys for sit down," she pointed to three old automobile tyres resting behind them, each person picked one up and sat down on it.

They struck up a conversation. A young man emerged from the bamboo hut and sat down beside Mabel. He was Mabel's partner, and they lived together in the hut. Mawu recognized him as the same person she had seen the previous evening mixing a white substance into a container.

"This be my boyfriend, Solo," Mabel introduced him.

"Lina resembles you more," Mawu smiled.

"Yes, because he is not Lina's biological father." Mabel replied.

"So where is her biological father, forgive my curiosity?"

"I was sixteen when I found out I was pregnant - three months along, to be exact. Crazy thing is, I had my period like normal for the first two months, so I had no idea. My mom suspected something was up, but I kept denying it because I wasn't missing periods. But then I started peeing all the time and my boobs got way bigger, so she took me to the hospital to get checked out. That's when the doctor told me I was three months pregnant! I was totally confused, like, how did this even happen if I was still getting my period? But apparently, it's possible - who knew?

My parents were totally blindsided when they found out I was pregnant. They'd always been super strict about who I hung out with, especially guys. I was a second-year student in senior high, studying general arts, and they barely let me socialize outside of school. But then there was Edem - he worked at a store near my school, and we'd chat whenever I stopped by. He was really friendly and always made me laugh. One time, he even asked me out when I went in to buy a calculator! Anyway, when my parents asked who the dad was, I told them it was Edem. They were shocked. I used to see him every day after school, since I finished classes at 3 pm and our driver would come pick me up..

One time, our driver was running late, so I got to hang out with Edem at his shop for a bit. We were flirting and joking around, and then we shared a passionate kiss. We snuck into the bathroom in the back of the store for some privacy, and that's where things went further. Honestly, my first time was pretty rough, it didn't feel amazing like my friends had said it would. But when I talked to them about it, they told me that's normal, and it gets better. So, I tried again, and it was totally different - it felt beautiful and empowering, like I was embracing my femininity and overcoming my shyness."

"Did you feel like you could stand up to your mom more after that? I've heard that can happen to girls after their first time, like they feel more confident and assertive." Adjei grinned.

Mabel paused and chuckled at Adjei's comment, and elicited laughter from both Mawu and Adjei. With a warm smile, she continued speaking, her words flowing smoothly.

"Yeah, I felt pretty mature after being with Edem a few times... But then he just up and left his job and went back to his hometown. I had no way of reaching him because my parents were so strict. I didn't even know he was gone until I got back to school and saw some new girl working at the store. I asked her about Edem, and she said she was new. I felt so lost and sad when I realized I'd never see him again. When I told my parents about the pregnancy, they freaked out and asked where Edem was. But I had no idea. They told me to leave and find him myself, which was crazy. I was so scared and alone. I went back to the store where Edem used to work, hoping to find some answers, but the owner couldn't help me. I ended up sleeping on the streets that night, getting soaked in the rain. It was freezing and miserable. The next morning, I wandered around looking for a place to go and found this old, abandoned building. I cleaned it up a bit and made it my own. It's not great, but at least I have a place to stay."

"Hey, how did you survive on your own in such a tough neighborhood? Did your parents set up a bank account for you or something, so you could get some cash when you needed it?" Mawu got curious.

"I had no money, no bank account, nothing. So I had to get creative. I went to the roadside and met these water vendors who sell sachets in traffic. One of them took me to their supplier and I started selling too. I made about 10gh a day, which was enough to get by. You were right, it was tough being new in a poor area. Life was hard, and I was struggling. Sometimes I couldn't even afford two meals a day. I remember this one night, I was so hungry around 2am, all I wanted was a sour mango. It was that bad.

"An unripe mango?" Adjei's jaw dropped.

"Yeah, being pregnant can be tough, you know? Sometimes it makes you do weird things. I had to go out in the night to find what I was craving for. I was feeling weak and alone, but I made myself go out. It was dark and took me an hour, but I found this mango tree with unripe fruits. I was so grateful; I threw stones at the tree to get some down. I ate them right there and then went back to my place to rest.

Then, around my eighth month, I met Solo. I was in this unfinished building, and I heard someone coming. I was scared, but then Solo showed up and told me to be quiet. He hid with me for a bit. Then he asked me to check if anyone was outside. I didn't want to, but I did, and no one was there. Turns out, Solo had stolen a phone and was hiding from the owner. He felt bad for me being alone and pregnant, so he decided to stick with me. He's a bit of a troublemaker, but he's been with me since then."

"Did your parents ever look for you when you were going through that tough time? I mean, I'm sure your mom knew how hard it was for you during your pregnancy - the sleepless nights, the weird feelings, and the uncertainty that comes with it. Did she ever come to comfort or support you?" Mawu inquired, her curiosity piqued by the anguish evident in Mabel's eyes.

Mabel handed Lina over to Solo and then pulled out a box of cigarettes from her pocket. She opened it, extracted a cigarette, and asked Solo for a lighter. After lighting up, she inhaled deeply and exhaled smoothly through her nostrils, releasing a slender stream of smoke. She continued...

"Honestly, my parents were never really there for me, and they still aren't. I'm not even sure I'd call them parent, you know? They never made an effort to find me or support me, even when I was pregnant and struggling. I mean, I was literally almost fainting in my ninth month, and Solo was unemployed too, so we were barely scraping by. We were so broke; we were worried about where our next meal would come from. But then we stumbled upon this cornfield near our place, and that's what kept us going. I didn't even get prenatal care, can you believe it? We just couldn't afford it. And Lina was born in the unfinished house we were living in, with no assistance from a midwife or any health worker. Mawu, it was really tough.

Solo went to town to try to find some money for food, but I was left to face the darkest part of childbirth alone. It's like every woman's worst nightmare - that moment when life and death hang in the balance. With each push, I felt like I was staring death in the eye, my heart pounding, my body screaming in agony. I could feel my body stretching, trying to accommodate this tiny human who was fighting to come into the world. But the pain was too much, and I was alone, completely alone, with no one to turn to, no one to hear my cries for help..."

"God was with you then," Adjei said while tears dropped from his eyes.

"God? Really? You still believe in that?" lights another cigarette. "I grew up hearing about how He's all-loving, all-knowing, all-powerful... but it's hard to take when you've seen the darkness I've seen. He just watched as my parents threw me out, left me to suffer on my own, and still don't seem to care that things have only gotten worse. And it's not just me - my friend Abena was raped and brutalized, and God just sat there, doing nothing. What kind of God is that? A God who doesn't care, or one who's just not capable of doing anything? Don't get me wrong, if you still believe in all that, that's your thing... but for me, it's just not enough." She said with fervor in her gaze.

Mabel continued to smoke, inhaling and exhaling slowly. Meanwhile, tears welled up in Mawu's eyes, and with a single blink, they streamed down her cheeks. Mawu couldn't help but think that situations can change people's lives, altering their beliefs, values, and actions. She was shocked to hear Mabel, a devoted Christian, speak disparagingly about God. In her youth, Mabel had been deeply committed to her faith, never joking about her bible studies. She had even led morning devotion and evening thanksgiving prayers at home, with her father's encouragement. At church she had headed the Sunday school class, often preaching sermon to her peers when the teacher allowed it. The pastors and congregants had loved her for her dedication to church activities.

"I don't know how, but I summoned every last bit of strength to keep going. I told myself, 'I can't die yet.' I was so tired, my breath was slipping away, and my vision was fading to black. I felt my soul tearing away from my body. And then, I heard this tiny cry, 'ngerr', and I knew my baby was finally here. But I was in a daze, thinking, 'how do I even cut the cord?' That's when I remembered the razor blade in my bag, so I grabbed it and cut the cord. Then I tied it off, trying to stop the bleeding. It was a moment of pure chaos, but I made it through."

"I'm really curious. How did you know all this? Did you somehow anticipate that you wouldn't make it to the hospital and prepare yourself? I mean, it's not like you had any experience with childbirth before. I'm genuinely impressed by your resourcefulness. So, what's the story? How did you know what to do at that moment?" Mawu expressed surprise as she sat attentively to listen to Mabel.

"Honestly, nobody taught me anything. I just figured it out as I went along. I think that's the thing about women - we've got this innate creativity that kicks in when things get tough. Necessity is the mother of invention, right? So, I gave birth to Lina in the middle of all this chaos, without any help or divine intervention or whatever. And you know what? At that moment, I just knew what to do. I felt the placenta come out, and I was relieved, but I was also exhausted. The room was a mess, and Lina was crying, but... I don't know, it was just this sense of joy and peace. I was too tired to even move, so I just lay there in the blood with Lina on top of me. And then I put her on my breast, and she stopped crying and started nursing. It was like this moment of pure instinct, you know?"

"I was fast asleep when Solo came back from town, holding this big white polythene bag. He looked like he'd seen a ghost or something. I tried to smile, but I was so weak. He just looked at me with this mix of shock and love, and then he sprang into action. He got water from the river, cleaned me and the baby, and even scrubbed the room clean. He brought me food too - kenkey and fish - and I was so starving, I just ate and slept again."

She lit her last cigarette and took a long drag. "I don't even want to think about everything we've been through with Lina. It's just too much. I know smoking is bad for me but sometimes, I just need something to calm my nerves. And my parents... they're just so fake. They care more about what others think than about me and my happiness. They preach about love and Jesus, but they don't even show me love." Adjei and Mawu were emotional, Mawu's tears flowed uncontrollably, as if she had chili pepper in her eyes.

"Our lives are our own to shape and mold. We're the masters of our fate, the architects of our own paths. Our parents and mentors can offer guidance, but ultimately, we're the ones who decide what happens next. By choosing to live a life of purpose and integrity, we honor ourselves and show those who doubted us that we're capable of achieving greatness. Yes, the pain of parental betrayal runs deep, but we can't let it define us. We have the power to create our own destiny, just like God created the world from nothing. We just need to tap into that power, stay focused, and never give up hope, even in the darkest times." Mawu expressed as she delicately brushed away the tears that cascaded down her cheeks with the back of her hands.

Solo gazed at Mawu's face and offered a smile as he skillfully rolled a marijuana joint in a pristine sheet of paper. With a flick of a lighter, he lit the tip and inhaled deeply, savoring the sensation of the smoke, akin to pepper dancing on his palate. A subtle grimace crossed his features as he shook his head in a rhythmic motion, lost in thought Contemplating the slender joint nestled between his fingers, he delicately tapped the center, causing the charred remnants at the end to disperse gracefully.

"Ha! You sound like one of those motivational speakers, you would soon tell me you built a water company with just a teardrop." Solo chuckled and shook his head. "Seriously though, who do you know in this neighborhood who's actually made it out? You're just taking painkillers for your stomach ulcer and spouting clichés. Let me tell you, my story. When I was a kid, my mom and I moved to Dansoman and stayed there until I was ten. But here's the thing - she never introduced me to any of our relatives, so I had no idea they even existed. I remember asking her about my dad once, and she got so angry, told me to never ask about him again. So, I never asked about my grandparents either, didn't want to get in trouble. My mom used to sell plantain chips on the street, and I'd sit under this makeshift shelter next to a guy doing mobile money transactions. When she was done, we'd head home. That's when she met a man, and he asked us to move in with him. We were living in a lottery kiosk at the time, so the thought of a real home was amazing to us."

Solo paused, taking a moment to draw from his marijuana. He ran his fingers through his hair and shook his head in a repetitive manner then resumed his narration. "So, after a month or so, the man started getting weird about me being around. He'd always say stuff like, 'I don't want him here' and 'Can't he go somewhere else?' And my mom would try to figure out what to do. Then, she met this other dude who took care of cattle and needed help. She thought, 'Okay, this is the solution' - I'll go live with him and work with the cattle, and then she and her boyfriend can have their space."

I worked with this dude for almost nine months when I got the news that my mom had passed away. I rushed to the house, but she was already gone - they'd taken her body to the morgue. I never got to say goodbye. And the thing is, I don't even know if she was ever buried properly. My mom had mentioned a sister once, showed me a picture, but said she was no longer alive. So, I had no one to turn to. The dude I worked with took me to my stepdad's place after I survived the ordeal of consuming a poison - the same guy my mom was living with when she died. Speaking of which, I almost died myself not long before that. I was out grazing the cattle one morning when I found this container under a palm tree. It smelled like palm wine, so I took a sniff and drank some. Big mistake. My stomach went crazy, and I passed out. Next thing I knew, I was waking up in my benefactor's house, soaked in water. He was freaked out and took me straight back to my stepdad's place." he quipped.

"My childhood was rough, Mawu. I was just 10 or 11 when my stepdad kicked me out after only three days. No help, no nothing. So, I had to hit the streets to find food. And, charlie, the things I've been through since then... it's crazy. I got into some bad stuff, sold drugs to survive. I'm talking cocaine and marijuana... But weirdly, I never got caught. Maybe it was because I looked so young and rough around the edges. But, for real, I saw some wild stuff. Like this one time, a guy got stabbed right in front of me. He forgot some drugs on a bus and came to report to the boss that he'd lost his drugs, and... just like that, he was gone. I was shocked, Mawu. My knee buckled, and I was done. I used to sleep in front of this store, but after that, I never went back. Too many bad vibes, you feel me?"

"Mawu," Solo drew in the smoke and released it through his lips, "Charlie, I've been through some wild stuff, you know? This ghetto is like a never-ending party - every day's a celebration, but not in a good way. It's like, we're always reminded that life's short, you feel me? But instead of getting all caught up in thinking about how messed up things are, we just live in the moment. We make the most of every second, because that's all we got."

Solo offered his joint to Mawu, who shook his head. Then he offered it to Adjei, who also declined. "Come on, guys, it's good stuff!" Solo said with a smile.

CHAPTER SIX

THE PAINFUL AUDITION

Asea of hopefuls flooded the registration area, each eager to showcase their unique talents to the judges. Amidst the crowd, Mawu and Adjei drew attention for their disheveled appearance, sparking curious glances from onlookers who perceived them as eccentric in their fashion choices. The ever-vigilant security guard approached the duo, inquiring about their purpose and ensuring the safety and order of the event. Mawu, with a calm and determined demeanor, clarified her intention to audition, her eyes betraying a mix of nervousness and resolve. Following the security guard's instructions, she joined the queue of participants, her mind abuzz with anticipation and excitement. Meanwhile, Adjei found a humble plastic chair beneath a canopy, patiently waiting for Mawu as the event's bustling activities swirled around him.

As Mawu waited in line to showcase her talents, she noticed the young lady in front of her wrinkle her nose in discomfort, subtly covering it in response to an unpleasant odor. Mawu realized with embarrassment that the smell was coming from her own attire, which she had worn for three consecutive days due to the water supply disruption in her area for the past week. Despite the challenges, Mawu's resilience shone through as she made the most of limited resources, using sachet water to clean herself in a makeshift way, focusing on her underarms and private areas.

Feeling a pang of unease at the young lady's reaction, Mawu silently vowed to endure the situation with grace and dignity, refusing to let external circumstances dampen her spirit or hinder her pursuit of showcasing her talents. The bustling atmosphere of the competition venue showcased Mawu's inner strength and perseverance, a testament to her unwavering dedication to her craft despite facing adversity. As the day unfolded with its twists and turns, Mawu's journey towards realizing her dreams continued, fueled by a resilient spirit that refused to be deterred by temporary challenges.

The registration had ended, and the audition was about to begin. The judges took their seats and the host formally introduced them to the audience. Each participant had been assigned a unique identification number during registration. As their numbers were called, participants would confidently take the stage, ready to showcase their unique talent to the audience and judges

"You're not here to compete with others, just show them what you've got! " Adjei gently tapped Mawu's shoulder.

"You know how I do it," Mawu smiled.

"Number 65!" One of the judges announced.

Many of the talents had auditioned. It was Mawu's turn. Mawu exuded confidence as she stepped onto the stage, her presence commanding attention from the very start. With a calm and composed demeanor, she walked with a purpose, her feet carrying her towards her destiny with unwavering certainty. Her head held high, she gazed out at the audience with a fierce determination in her eyes; her smile radiating a sense of self-assurance that was impossible to ignore. Every step she took seemed to declare, 'I am here, I am ready, and I am unstoppable.' The surrounding air seemed to vibrate with an energy that was both captivating and intimidating, as if she was a force to be reckoned with. As she took her place at the microphone, the room seemed to hold its collective breath, waiting to see what she would do next. As she unleashed a powerful melody, a hush fell over the audience, captivated by her performance. The judges, utterly engrossed, were taken aback by the sheer potency of Mawu's vocal prowess. One of them nodded in rhythmic approval as she serenaded the room with her enchanting voice.

"This lady is already a star," one judge remarked to another, impressed by her exceptional talent and captivating stage presence..

The three judges rose to their feet and applauded Mawu as she concluded her final melodic note.

"Thank you," Mawu smiled graciously as she gracefully approached Adjei, and embraced him warmly.

"Wow, Mawu, you were absolutely amazing out there! You totally owned that stage and showed them who you are. I loved how you worked the judges. You could tell they were eating it up!"

"Thank you bro, I enjoyed the performance myself."

The initial phase of the audition process was completed, and the top twenty candidates was identified. These individuals would proceed to the next stage of auditions, where the field would be further reduced to the final five contestants. "Attention, please," one of the judges called.

Everywhere was hushed as anticipation filled the air, with every individual eagerly awaiting the sound of their own name. A palpable tension enveloped the room, hearts quickened their pace, and mouths grew dry with nerves. All eyes were fixed on the judge, who held the list of names in hand. With each name the judge called out, a wave of relief and joy washed over those fortunate enough to be selected. The judge reached the fifteenth name, and only five spots remained to be filled. Adjei was on edge, anxiously awaiting the mention of Mawu's name, while Mawu remained composed, exuding a sense of calm. Despite her own anticipation, she graciously smiled at those whose names had already been called.

"Hey, Adjei, chill out, bro," Mawu said softly, trying to calm him down. "You're going to wear a hole in the floor pacing like that. Just take a deep breath and relax, okay?"

"Charlie, you totally crushed it out there! You even out-sang that girl they're all raving about," Adjei said, nodding towards one girl in a green dress who was chatting with a group of friends. "I mean, she's getting all the hype, but you were way better."

"As the judge said, the names are listed in a random sequence."

"Mawu Johnson!" the judge mentioned.

Adjei jumped in excitement and hugged Mawu tightly.

"Oh yes, I just know you will make it! Yes, yes, yes! I felt it! You've made it, Mawu, I was sure of it!" Adjei exclaimed, bouncing up and down with enthusiasm.

"Distinguished guests, the wait is over! We proudly present the top twenty finalists selected for their exceptional talent and dedication. These individuals will compete for a coveted record deal with our prestigious label partners. Congratulations to the finalists! To those who didn't make the cut, we appreciate your participation and encourage you to pursue future opportunities.

Finalists, please proceed to the stage to draw your performance number. This moment is yours to seize. Showcase your artistry and make it unforgettable. Thank you, and good luck!"

After the ballot, they were granted a twenty-minute respite to prepare themselves for the impending audition. Mawu and Adjei opted to seize the opportunity to satiate their hunger, as they had abstained from food since morning. They ventured to a nearby local eatery to buy food. Upon arrival, they noticed only three individuals in line. Mawu joined the queue while Adjei settled on a nearby bench.

"Hey Amelia, I thought we agreed on 5 cedis for the waakye, 2 cedis for the talia, and 2 cedis for the gari? But this waakye doesn't look like it's worth 5 cedis, you know? It's a bit skimpy, if you ask me." The first buyer complained.

"Hey, it's not me being stingy, okay? Things have gotten really expensive in the market lately. If I keep using the same old ladle measurements, I'll be selling at a loss. I got to adjust somehow, please."

Mawu signaled Adjei to come.

"I only have ten cedis on me, and honestly, six cedis for waakye is going to leave us hanging. We need more food than that, "Mawu whispered, leaning in close.

"I've only got 2 cedis, but I'm thinking, let's get two plates for 6 cedis each. That way, we'll have plenty. If we get one plate for

12 cedis, she'll probably shortchange us on the serving, you feel me?"

"Yeah, that's a great idea! Let's do it," Mawu said with a grin.

In a short while, Mawu joined Adjei at the table carrying the meal. They commenced dining while engaging in conversation. Their discussion revolved around the dilemma of returning home due to their depleted funds for transportation. Mawu felt a hit on her back.

"Oh sorry, I'm so sorry please forgive me," Stella inadvertently struck Mawu's back with her left hand.

"Aw, don't worry, please! It's just a minor hit. I'm good," Mawu said, flashing a calming smile.

"Mind if I squeeze in next to you?" Stella asked, juggling a plate of waakye in one hand.

"Sure! Why not?" Mawu smiled.

Stella sat down to savor her meal. She was a young woman in her early twenties, and exuded a captivating beauty with her fair complexion and radiant smile. Her plate was adorned with a delightful array of proteins and vegetables, hinting at her refined taste. Clad in a luxurious pink "Adidas" tracksuit paired with pristine white "Adidas" sneakers, she exuded an air of sophistication and elegance.

"Hey, take this, you guys need it," Stella said picking a fish from her plate and handling it to Mawu.

"Nah, we're almost finished, thanks!" Mawu said with a smile.

"I insist."

Mawu accepted the fish and thanked Stella. Adjei thanked Stella too.

"I can tell you're a really kind person, you know? Not like some others who don't even care about people like us," Adjei said, shaking his head in appreciation.

"I feel like we're all connected on some level, but life experiences make us who we are, right? And wow, you were absolutely mesmerizing on stage - your energy and vibe were infectious! By the way, I'm Stella."

"I'm Mawu, thanks for the love! That means a lot to me."

"Hey, I'm Adjei. Mawu's voice coach and manager, aka the guy who puts up with her diva moments."

"No way, a voice coach? That's amazing! But hey, manager extraordinaire, can you hook me up with some new kicks? My shoes are dying over here!"

"Haha, guess I can't brag in peace no more!" Adjei chuckled, cracking up the group.."Okay, girls, let's roll out! Audition awaits!"

The second round of auditions was underway. Mawu was slotted at number 8 while Stella was assigned number 15. As the first contestant finished his performance, the second participant took the stage. commanding attention with his striking appearance and soulful voice. His enchanting melody mesmerized the audience, and his charismatic presence was spellbinding, even without eye contact.

However, despite the captivating performance, Mawu felt uneasy. She experienced a sudden discomfort in her abdomen and an unfamiliar sensation in her rectum. The urge to use the restroom became overwhelming, but she was determined to audition first, giving the 10-minute walk to the facility. She tried to hold on, but nature called, and she hastily made her way to the restroom. To her surprise, she run into Adjei emerging from the gentlemen's lavatory.

Adjei quipped, "Ha! You've got a case of the runs too, huh?

Mawu was too flustered to respond, so she hastily made her way to the women's restroom. Just as she was about to slip inside, she spotted Stella emerging from one of the stalls.

"You're having a runaway stomach too?" Mawu said and hastily entered a stall.

Stella stepped out of the restroom and caught sight of Adjei lounging on a nearby rock

"Hey, did you come with Mawu?"

"Nah, I was already here when she showed up," Adjei replied.

"You mean you're running too? What's going on, is it something we ate?"

"Could it be the waakye? Ugh, I need to go again," Adjei said, hurrying back to the restroom.

Stella's stomach started churning again. She felt the all-too-familiar urge to dash to the restroom.She wondered how they would make it through the audition if their digestive issues didn't let up. Finally, she couldn't wait any longer and rushed to the restroom, only to find all three stalls taken. She lightly knocked on the door where Mawu was, hoping to hurry her along.

"Mawu, almost done in there?"

"Stella, you're kidding me, right? You just left!" Mawu said, incredulous.

"Mawu, hurry up! I'm about to burst!" Stella said, her voice laced with desperation.

Mawu hurriedly exited the stall, allowing Stella to rush in. The relieved sound of Stella's body releasing its contents made it clear that she had barely made it in time, a few seconds longer and she would have had an accident.

"Stella, I'll be outside, waiting for you. Let's go together. I'm sure Adjei is still lingering around, waiting for us."

"Adjei's headed back to the men's restroom, so you should go to the audition center now, Mawu! I'm number 15, so they'll call you before me. Go, go, go!" Stella urged..

"Alright, I'm off to the audition! Meet me there with Adjei when you're done, okay?" Mawu called out as she rushed away.

Upon arriving at the audition grounds, she felt a slight tingling sensation in her lower abdomen and a twinge of discomfort. The urge to use the restroom resurfaced. Despite her reluctance to make a second trip, her body's insistent signals left her no choice but to return to the restroom to avoid potential embarrassment. As she made her way back, she encountered Stella and Adjei.

"You're heading back to the restroom again?" Adjei said, sounding surprised.

"I got to."

"Hey, I'm going to send Adjei to grab some meds from the pharmacy, so hurry back, okay?" Stella said.

Mawu left in haste. Adjei promptly proceeded to the pharmacy, located directly across from the audition venue, and obtained the prescribed medication. Meanwhile, Stella patiently awaited her turn for the audition. Number 12 was currently on stage showcasing her talent, indicating that Mawu had missed the chance to audition. Shortly after, Adjei returned with the medication and warm water. Having already taken his dose, he administered Stella's medication as per the pharmacist's instructions. When it was Stella's turn, she proceeded to audition. Adjei felt a sense of unease and disappointment, convinced that Mawu would have secured a spot among the top five finalists if she had auditioned. It was disheartening to see another missed opportunity.

Mawu returned to find that the audition had concluded. A judge announced the names of the individuals who had secured a spot in the final five. Overcome with emotion, Mawu burst into tears, with cascades of tears streaming down her cheeks. Adjei approached and enveloped her in a comforting embrace.

"Hey, this too shall pass, okay?" Adjei said with a gentle smile.

Mawu also offered a gentle smile. Although Stella's name was not among the final five, she gracefully concealed her disappointment behind a facade of elegance. Mawu and Adjei warmly embraced her, expressing their gratitude for her compassionate nature.

"I'll catch you guys later, I'm thinking of heading to the market soon," Stella said with a wave.

CHAPTER SEVEN

THE RAPE ATTEMPT

Adjei was in the midst of his market colleagues' chatter when he caught wind of an intriguing topic: a music producer who had recently taken up residence in their neighborhood. Intrigued by the news, he promptly joined the conversation to learn more. It was a common sight to see Adjei actively seeking out opportunities for his talented friend, Mawu. His unwavering belief in her musical abilities fueled his determination to see her succeed. To Adjei, Mawu was not just a friend but a cherished big sister whom he vowed to protect at all costs. Despite the mere three-month age gap between them, Adjei held Mawu in high regard, always envisioning a bright future for her in the music industry. Their bond was a testament to the power of friendship and support in pursuing dreams.

"Who be dis producer you dey refer to, and which side him dey work for?" Adjei inquire, in a pidgin language.

"Luzii, him studio dey next to dat Vodafone pole wey dey railway," one of them replied.

Luzii, a former inmate, had relocated from Jamestown to Nungua, a suburb of Accra, after facing discrimination. He had been convicted of unintentionally causing the death of a friend during a heated dispute. Both individuals had been involved in illicit drug activities in the neighborhood, and a quarrel arose one day over the division of money. Suspecting Luzii of deceit, his friend, in a fit of rage, aimed a firearm at him. In a quick turn of events, Luzii gestured as though someone was approaching from behind his friend, prompting the latter to shift his gaze. Seizing the opportunity, Luzii firmly grasped the firearm and his friend's hand, engaging in a struggle to disarm him. This culminated in a fatal shot, and his friend fell to the ground, clutching his chest. After enduring a decade behind bars, Luzii had returned from incarceration to carve out a livelihood in the outside world.

"How you guys take know am," Adjei further asked.

"Tommy go studio yesterday, record him song, and you go like am, him sound dey sweet!"

"I believe say he dey support talents, sekof I wan go there plus Mawu?"

"You fit ask am for him side."

Early the next day, Adjei set off for Luzii's studio. Situated in the ghetto, the studio's exterior was unassuming, but upon entering, one was met with a sight of extraordinary beauty. The studio was adorned with blue, red, violet, and yellow LED lights that harmonized perfectly with the ambiance, creating a profoundly soothing atmosphere. Luzii's living space consisted of a chamber and a hall, with the latter of which was utilized as his studio.

"Good morning boss," Adjei greeted.

"Yoo sup, how you bee, you dey come do recording?" He spoke in pidgin.

"Please, no be so. My sister be musician, she need help. Abeg, you dey support artists wey no get money for recording?"

"No be everybody."

"Me understand, but Mawu be talented pass, you know? For dat last audition wey dem hold for Teshie Gornor school, she go perform and everybody shock! She for enter final five, but dat bad food wey we chop spoil everything!"

"Oh, so that fine girl be your sister?"

"Yes, she be my sister."

"Oh okay, what be your name?"

"My name be Adjei, and I dey reside for this ghetto too."

"You from the Ga tribe?"

"Yes, I be Ga."

"I know say Mawu na Ewe name, but how Mawu wey be Ewe take become sister to Adjei wey be Ga?"

"Wen I talk say she be my sister, I no mean say we get same mama and papa. But still, you for know say for Ghana here, inter-tribal marriage dey happen plenty. Like our former president, Jerry John Rawlings, wey be Ewe, him marry Nana Konadu Agyemang, wey be Ashanti. Dem daughters get names wey show say dem mix culture - one be Zenator, wey be Ewe name, another be Asantewaa, wey be Ashanti name. So, you see say inter-tribal influence dey our society."

"I hear. Make you come plus your sister morro," Luzii said, and Adjei thanked him..

In the afternoon at the bustling market, Adjei excitedly shared with Mawu his recent visit to the music producer. Mawu's face lit up with joy upon hearing the news, and they quickly made plans to visit Luzii's studio later that evening, after they finished their activities at the market.

After wrapping up their day at the market, they headed home, where they freshened up by taking refreshing baths and changing into more comfortable clothes. Then, they set off to Luzii's studio. Upon arrival, they were greeted by the sound of music coming from the studio, indicating that Luzii was in the middle of a recording session.

Adjei and Mawu waited patiently for Luzii to finish his current recording, after which they could engage with him. As they listened to the captivating beats and melodies, they couldn't help but nod their heads in rhythm with the music, thoroughly enjoying the experience. Finally, Luzii wrapped up the recording and turned his attention to Adjei and Mawu, greeting them with a warm smile. He was now ready to interact with them and discuss their plans. The studio atmosphere was electric with creativity and excitement.

"Yoo sup, what dey go on?" Luzii asked in his characteristic pidgin dialect.

Mawu and Adjei were not taken aback by Luzii's inquiry, as a Ghanaian proverb resonates: "We may already possess the knowledge, yet we seek confirmation."

"I come here dis morning to talk about my sister, wey you say make I go bring am, dat be why I come plus her this evening."

"Okay I barb... What be your name?" Luzii turned to Mawu.

"My name is Mawu."

"Come stand at the back of the mic and give me Acapella make I hear."

Mawu positioned herself behind the microphone, donned the headset, and delivered a captivating acapella performance that sent shivers down Luzii's spines. Luzii was captivated by her melodious voice and promptly expressed interest in collaborating with her. He extended an open invitation to Mawu to visit his studio whenever her schedule permitted. Adjei and Mawu expressed their gratitude before departing for home, elated with happiness.

A Few days later, Mawu visited Luzii at his studio with a song she had written. It was morning, and the sun had risen, casting a creative energy over the studio that always sparked between them. As Mawu handed Luzii the lyrics she had poured her heart into, her eyes lit up. They both knew this was the beginning of something special. As they sat down to work on the song, Mawu's voice filled the room with raw emotion and talent. Each note she sang seemed to breathe life into the words she had written. Meanwhile, Luzii, with his keen sense of rhythm, crafted a beat that perfectly complemented Mawu's vocals.

Creating a beat and recording a song is no easy feat; it requires patience, dedication, and a lot of trial and error. Mawu sang the chorus repeatedly, trying to find the perfect cadence that would elevate the song to another level. As the hours passed, Mawu's stomach started to growl; she had only eaten a light breakfast of "Millet Porridge" and "Akala" with Adjei before coming to the studio. Adjei, her ever-supportive friend, had stayed behind to sell goods at the market so they would have money for food later.

Feeling the hunger pangs, Luzii suggested they take a break. He disappeared into his kitchen and emerged with a steaming plate of rice, which was a welcome respite after hours of arduous work. As they sat together to share the simple meal, it tasted like a feast. They shared not just the food but also a sense of accomplishment. Just as they were about to dig in, a sudden knock on the door interrupted their moment.

'Who be that?" Luzii shouted.

"Bossu ibi me," the person replied in pidgin.

He pushed open the door and entered. It was a gentleman who had arrived to resume recording his track.

"Yoo man come make we chop," Luzii invited him.

"Oh, bossu make you continue, me sef I make full already, charlie big ups."

He expressed his gratitude to Luzii and requested that they continue, as his appetite had been satiated. Luzii instructed Mawu to finish the remaining food while he washed his hands and attended to the gentleman. Meanwhile, Luzii accessed the gentleman's file on the computer and began his work. After completing her meal, Mawu proceeded to the veranda, where she meticulously cleaned the dishes and organized everything methodically. Aware that she had to depart and return the following day to resume her tasks, she thanked Luzii for the meal before taking her leave.

The gentleman quipped in pidgin, "Luzii, this fine girl, she be your chick?"

"Yeah, na my small girl that," Luzii replied.

The gentleman praised Mawu's beauty, "She dey bee oo."

Mawu arrived at the bustling market, where she coincidentally ran into Adjei. Excitedly, she shared with Adjei the thrilling news about her recording sessions. As they strolled through the market, Mawu couldn't contain her enthusiasm, describing in vivid detail the delicious meal Luzii had prepared for her before she left the studio.

Adjei listened attentively, but his expression turned slightly guarded when Mawu mentioned eating food cooked by Luzii. He gently voiced his concern, not out of jealousy but out of genuine care for Mawu's well-being. Adjei emphasized the importance of being cautious when consuming meals prepared by individuals whose background are unknown.

"Hey Mawu, please be careful okay. Don't eat anything from someone you don't know well, especially if you're alone with them in a room. I don't trust anyone except you, so you shouldn't trust anyone except me either. Are you still going to the studio tomorrow?"

"Yeah, we didn't finish up, so I'll head back tomorrow to wrap things up."

"Okay, listen, if you're hungry tomorrow when you're at the studio, just come meet me at the market and I'll grab you some food, okay? Please don't eat anything he offers you, I don't feel right about you being alone with him, to be honest."

"Adjei, chill! I can handle myself, I'll be careful, don't stress about it."

The following day, Mawu had dressed up and was about to leave for Luzii's studio when Adjei called her from inside their humble abode, where they had managed to secure a kiosk to stay in overnight. They no longer seek refuge in abandoned vehicles.

"Hey, you're taking off already?" Adjei asked.

"Yep, stay safe in the market, I'll try to get there early to give you a hand," Mawu said.

"Seriously, be careful and don't forget what I told you. You're going to the studio to record, not to snack. Just keep your focus and you'll be fine!," Adjei cautioned.

They left home together and parted ways at a junction, where they went their separate ways.

Luzii was repairing his motorcycle, seated on a sturdy wooden bench with a portable Bluetooth speaker beside him. He indulged in listening to melodies he had composed for emerging artists. As Mawu approached, he warmly greeted her, and received a beaming smile in return. Luzii invited Mawu to join him on the bench, and she gracefully took a seat beside him.

"Mawu, why you fine so?,Wetin be your secret?" Luzii smiled.

"Ibi god oo, boss," Mawu smiled back.

"I wan know the food wey you dey chop so say I go chop some. I wan become fine like you. Chai, your beauty no from here at all."

"I dey appreciate your kind words, boss," Mawu smiled.

While they conversed, Luzii repaired his motorcycle.. About twenty minutes later, he finished the task and started the engine. After verifying that everything was in working order, he carefully parked the motorcycle in front of his residence and secured it with a sturdy metallic chain and padlock to prevent theft. He then ushered Mawu into his foyer, which doubled as a studio, and gestured for her to take a seat while he accessed a folder on the computer. As he sat beside her in a chair next to the desktop, he prepared to showcase something. Once Mawu was settled, he played back the musical composition he had crafted the previous day.

"Wow, dis beat dey sweet me! You work am for night?" Mawu asked.

"Yes, I do am. Hope say you like am."

"Yes, I like am."

Mawu felt a surge of discomfort as she sensed Luzii's hand gliding along her thigh. She subtly shifted her position, creating some distance between them, while Luzii gazed into her eyes and offered a gentle smile.

"Make you no tell me say you be virgin."

"Abeg, I no like dis one, I dey respect you too much, I no expect dis kind thing from you, abeg."

"Me, I no dey help person like dat oo, you be fine girl, make you use wetin you get to get wetin you want."

"Abeg, if dis na your mind, den I dey sorry, I no need your help."

Mawu's heart began to race as fear gripped her, realizing the dangerous situation she was in. The sight of Luzii's exposed underwear sent shivers down her spine. Her urgency to escape intensified, knowing her virtue was at stake. She couldn't bear the thought of losing it in such a terrifying encounter with a man like Luzii.

As Luzii advanced towards her, Mawu's instincts kicked in, prompting her to take cautious steps backward. Her eyes scanned the dimly lit room for any possible means of defense or escape. Then, like a glimmer of hope in the darkness, she spotted a beer bottle lying under one of the chairs. Without hesitation, she swiftly picked it up, her hands trembling with a mix of fear and determination.

"Abeg stay back," Mawu warned Luzii.

Luzii was in an extremely altered state, consumed by intense feelings of lust for Mawu. He seemed to seek solace only in sleeping with her. Her cautions fell on deaf ears, as if Mawu was speaking a language he could not understand. He was like a wild lion hunting its prey, driven by primal instinct.

As Luzii advanced towards Mawu with intensity, she struggled to defend herself. In a desperate bid to protect herself, she used the beer bottle to strike him on the head, causing his vision to blur and momentarily disorienting him. Seizing the opportunity, Mawu pushed Luzii away and made a swift escape through the door. The encounter left its mark on her, evident in the torn dress and cuts on her skin, likely inflicted by his sharp nails during the struggle.

Mawu hurried to the market and recounted the incident to Adjei, who then accompanied her to the police station to file a formal complaint. This led to the arrest and apprehension of Luzii.

CHAPTER EIGHT

THE DEADLY MISTAKE

S tella, a young lady in her early twenties, possessed a captivating beauty that was accentuated by her curves and fair complexion. Her charming feature of dimples on both cheeks would appear whenever she smiled, adding a delightful touch to her overall appearance. Standing about five inches taller than her friend Mawu, Stella exuded a graceful presence that drew attention wherever she went. As an embodiment of African beauty standards, she had beautifully sculpted calves that enhanced her allure.

One couldn't help but notice Stella's large, enchanting eyes, which seemed to hold a world of emotions within them. They were like windows to her soul, reflecting her inner warmth and kindness. When she gazed at you, it felt as though she was peering into your very essence, making you feel truly seen and understood. Stella's eyes had a way of illuminating her face, making her beauty even more radiant and captivating. Her infectious smile and kind heart were just a few of the qualities that made her truly special.

Stella was not just a young lady of beauty and grace; she embodied a radiant combination of inner and outer beauty. Her presence was like a breath of fresh air, bringing joy and light to all those fortunate enough to know her. Stella was a gem among gems, a true embodiment of African beauty in every sense of the word.

It was around noon when one of Mawu and Adjei's male friends escorted Stella to meet them beneath a bamboo canopy in the bustling market. The sight of Stella brought immense joy to Mawu and Adjei, who had doubted she would visit. Adorned in elegant attire, Stella captivated the attention of those around her, who couldn't help but sneak glances in her direction. As promised during the audition, Stella had paid them a surprise visit. Mawu graciously invited her to take a seat on the bench, initiating a profound conversation. They delved into their musical journey, reflecting on the progress made thus far. As Mawu shared the challenges she faced in her musical pursuits, shedding light on the stagnation she encountered, a sense of compassion washed over Stella.

Stella informed Mawu of her desire to travel to Dubai together, highlighting the potential financial gains that could support Mawu's music career. She mentioned visiting her generous friends in Dubai, expressing confidence that they would be willing to offer assistance once they heard her story. Mawu was thrilled at the prospect of experiencing Dubai firsthand. Although Adjei was happy for Mawu, he harbored reservations about her travel plans. However, Mawu reassured him, promising to return with newfound opportunities to improve their lives through the assistance of Stella's benevolent friends.

Two weeks after Stella's visit to the market, she presented Mawu with the ticket and accommodation, informing her of their upcoming week-long escapade to revel in Dubai's allure and splendor.

Upon their arrival in Dubai, Mawu found herself utterly captivated and entranced by the country's magnificence. The thought of residing in such a country for the remainder of her days ignited a profound desire within her. "Every facet gleams with a sense of grandeur," she mused softly to herself. A profound sense of contentment enveloped her being as she made a conscious effort to feast her eyes upon the sights, ensuring she had an abundance of tales to recount upon their return to Ghana. Unless Adjei procured additional listeners, he would find himself lacking an audience to regale with her experience, much like a canoe navigating through the boundless sea of her encounters without a crew.

On the third day after their arrival, Mawu was approached by an enigmatic gentleman whose demeanor clearly indicated his immense wealth. He expressed his admiration for Mawu and proposed spending an evening together in a tranquil setting. He also offered to compensate her for her time with a day of shopping at luxury stores of her choice and a substantial sum of fifty thousand dollars. Mawu was taken aback by the man's proposition, questioning its reality. Seeking counsel, she confided in Stella, who assured her that there was no cause for concern, as this was characteristic of the generosity displayed by billionaires in Dubai. Stella encouraged Mawu to envision the array of designer bags, accessories, and other luxuries she could acquire in a single day, along with the significant monetary reward, all in exchange for simply enjoying the gentleman's company. Unbeknownst to Mawu, a virgin and unfamiliar with the euphemism "have a good time," she innocently believed it entailed engaging in pleasant conversation in a sophisticated environment.

Mawu was taken aback by the substantial sum offered for mere companionship, yet she was swayed by Stella's assurance of the benevolence of her friends in Dubai. Her rendezvous with the gentleman was set for the following day. As dawn broke, a chauffeur arrived promptly at 10 am to escort her from her lodgings in a Bugatti La Voiture Noire. She was ushered to meet Mr. Ahmed, the gentleman who had requested her presence for the night, and was required to sign a non-disclosure agreement. Mr. Ahmed elucidated to Mawu the significance of her signature on the document, citing religious constraints and his desire for discretion regarding their interactions that evening. "Discretion? Does he think I'm prone to divulging confidences, should he choose to confide in me?" Mawu pondered to herself, her naivety evident in her thoughts. She remained oblivious to the unfolding events.

Mr. Ahmed handed a bag of money to the man who had picked Mawu up from her hotel. The man, who appeared more like a bodyguard, exuded a commanding presence with his well-built, muscular physique, towering height, thick beard, and fair complexion standing at approximately seven feet tall. Mr. Ahmed instructed him to accompany Mawu on a shopping trip and then presented her with a sizable envelope. She explored Dubai's prominent establishments, including restaurants, spas, colossal shopping centers, and various tourist attractions, indulging in a novel experience. Mawu purchased an authentic Chanel handbag, Hermes sandals, luxurious fragrances, Yves Saint Laurent apparel, Prada sneakers, Louis Vuitton wallets, Balenciaga items, and an array of other high-end brands. She also acquired stylish outfits for Adjei, allowing herself to drift into a daydream. After the shopping spree and sightseeing, the bodyguard escorted her back to her hotel, instructing her to prepare for a 10 pm rendezvous to attend to Mr. Ahmed's requirements.

She could not believe it; it felt almost surreal. The joy of her successful shopping spree filled her heart as she envisioned selling these prestigious brands to further her music career. The prospect of earning more money thrilled her, knowing she would have plenty to share with Adjei, whom she already missed dearly.

At 10 pm sharp, the bodyguard arrived to escort Mawu and accompany her to Mr. Ahmed's residence. They were stationed in his opulent seaside mansion, where they proceeded to the pier and embarked on an exquisitely crafted vessel, venturing out into the vast expanse of the ocean. Mr. Ahmed was not alone; there were four men with him, Mawu went straight to Mr. Ahmed and sat beside him. He asked her to remove her clothes. She was confused and began to panic; everything was unfolding differently than she had anticipated, and, it was more than she could handle that night. A virgin who had left home to work in the market and make her dreams come true was now about to compromise her values due to her naivety. Mawu had become their sexual object, the object of their sexual sadism that night.

The four gentlemen committed an egregious act against her, and subsequently, she was cast into the water. Mr. Ahmed then instructed his security man to retrieve her from the water, after which she was given a large, pristine towel to cover herself.

She visibly shook and cried uncontrollably, sensing discomfort in her intimate areas. She perceived a foul odor and checked into her hotel room around 4:00 a.m. in a state of utter distress and disgrace.

Stella entered Mawu's hotel suite around 9:00 a.m. to pay her a visit. "My dear, you will get through this," Stella reassured her with a warm smile. "What is wrong with Stella? She can see I'm devastated, and yet she still says stuff like that?" Mawu wondered.

"Why did you keep the truth from me? Why did you lie to me? You knew this was going to go down, didn't you?

"Not everyone is into that sort of thing, it's just about being intimate. Some people enjoy it, and honestly, I didn't want to say no because I didn't want you to loose goodies."

"What are you even talking about? You think life is all about fancy stuff and luxuries? Stella, you're a total monster! I'll never forgive you for this!" Mawu declared, her eyes flashing with a fierce glint.

"Come on, don't tell me you're okay with how you're living in that market? I'm trying to help you out and you're repaying me with insults? Can't you just be grateful for once?"

"I hate you, Stella!" Mawu exclaimed, and Stella stormed out of the room, clearly upset.

The seven days had passed, and they returned to Ghana. Adjei was delighted to see Mawu back, knowing she had brought something for him from Dubai. He was eager to hear about her experiences. However, Mawu seemed different since her return; she needed someone to confide in - someone who could empathize with her, someone she could trust.

She sat with Adjei alone under a tree in a serene corner of their neighborhood and recounted every detail of the incident to him. Adjei was left speechless and astounded for a moment, then he let out a deep sigh. Gazing into Mawu's eyes, he tightly embraced her, offering solace in his warm arms.

"Wow, Mawu, I'm so proud of you for staying strong through all this. You're incredibly brave and resilient. I'm honored to know you and grateful you're in my life. Don't worry, your secret is safe with me. I know things are tough right now, but I believe in you. You got this! Just keep pushing forward and don't give up" As tears welled up in Adjei's eyes, he imparted these heartfelt words of encouragement.

"Honestly, I don't know if I'll ever be ready for parenthood. I'm struggling to cope with my emotions right now. Suicidal thoughts are constantly haunting me, and it's pushing me to the edge. The quiet moments are the worst - the whispers in my head are relentless and drive me crazy. I'm barely holding on, and I'm scared of losing my grip. Sometimes I find myself screaming and crying for no reason, and it's like I'm rotting from the inside out. I appreciate your support and non-judgmental ear - I'm trying to come to terms with the mess I've made. I trusted the wrong people and let my ambition and greed consume me. I feel like I've sold my soul for nothing, and now I'm paying the price."

"Hey, Mawu, don't beat yourself up over this. You didn't know what you were getting into, and it's not like you were being greedy. Don't blame yourself, sis. You're stronger than this, and it's not going to break you. Just remember, this too shall pass, okay?" Adjei wrapped Mawu in a warm hug.

CHAPTER NINE

A WRONG DECISION

It had been several years since Mawu left her family home to wander the streets, leaving her whereabouts unknown to her concerned family. Surprisingly, her parents never sought the police's help in finding her, as Mawu had reassured her mother on the day of her departure that she wasn't missing. Despite this, the family longed for her return, hoping for a sign or a call from Mawu. The tension within the family was evident, with Mrs. Johnson holding her husband accountable for their daughter's departure. She believed that they had been too strict with Mawu, denying her the freedom to pursue her desired career path. In contrast, Mr. Johnson held a distinct perspective, feeling it was their duty as parents to guide their child toward a suitable career. He expressed concerns about Mawu's lack of dedication to her studies, fearing he would fail as a father if he did not push her to excel academically. The conflicting viewpoints within the family added to the emotional turmoil caused by Mawu's absence, leaving them all yearning for resolution.

However, Frank held a distinct perspective from his parents regarding Mawu's future career. He believed that talent and knowledge should underscore the importance of holistic personal development, emphasizing the need for individuals to pursue careers that align with their true passions and abilities. In contrast,

Mr. Johnson was insistent on imposing his own career choices on Mawu.

Frank's absence was deeply felt by his family, and his passing was a painful experience for them. The struggle to even locate his remains for a proper burial highlighted the profound impact of his loss.

At twenty-six, Suzzy found herself the sole remaining child in her family home. Her parents, devout members of their church, began to gently nudge her towards finding a partner within the church community. In their congregation, It was a common belief that marrying within the same faith was not just a preference, but a requirement outlined in the church's constitution. Suzzy had witnessed her friend, whom she had introduced to the church, embracing this tradition and finding happiness in marriage and motherhood.

In her final year at university, Suzzy met Peter, a young man who captured her heart. Despite his humble background, Peter's humility, dedication, and sincerity impressed Suzzy. His commitment to his studies and his mother's modest gari and beans business demonstrated his strong work ethic and sense of responsibility. Deeply enamored with Peter, Suzzy made a heartfelt promise to support him financially through his education, sharing both her resources and academic materials as they pursued the same program.

Their relationship blossomed, built on mutual respect and trust, as Peter remained steadfastly loyal to Suzzy despite the attention from other women. Suzzy's admiration for Peter's character continued to grow as she witnessed his perseverance and integrity in every aspect of his life. The bond they shared was founded on genuine care and support, with Suzzy's love propelling Peter towards his goals through unwavering encouragement. In a world where superficial attractions often cloud true connections, Suzzy and Peter's relationship shone brightly as a beacon of authenticity and devotion.

After graduating, Suzzy and Peter, two bright individuals with promising futures, secured jobs at prestigious banks, paving the way for their shared journey ahead. As they embarked on their professional lives, their personal relationship blossomed, weaving dreams of a life intertwined with love and ambition. However, amidst their growing closeness, Suzzy harbored a lingering hesitation: she had yet to introduce Peter, her beloved, to her parents.

One fateful evening, during a cozy family dinner, Suzzy mustered the courage to reveal Peter's existence to her parents. With a heart full of affection, she vividly described Peter's qualities and the love they shared. To her surprise and delight, her father, a man of few words but profound wisdom, gave his blessing for her to bring Peter home for a formal introduction.

As Peter arrived at Suzzy's doorstep; the air was thick with anticipation. He exuded warmth and respect, his physical appearance mirroring his inner character. With a dark complexion that bespoke resilience and a stature that commanded attention, he portrayed a man of strength. Noteworthy were his strikingly unique features, including his height of 5 feet and 8 inches and his captivating, natural pink lips that added a touch of charm to his demeanor.

Suzzy's heart danced with joy as Peter crossed the threshold into her family's abode. Her beaming smile mirrored the happiness radiating within her as she guided Peter to the dining table, where her parents awaited with eager curiosity. Mr. and Mrs. Johnson, embodiments of kindness and hospitality, welcomed Peter with open arms, making him feel like a cherished member of their family from the first exchange of words.

The evening unfolded as a tapestry of laughter, shared stories, and genuine conversations that seamlessly wove Peter into the fabric of Suzzy's family life. As the hours passed in a blur of engaging dialogue and heartfelt connections, Peter expressed his gratitude for the warm reception and the opportunity to be among such wonderful people. With a polite demeanor, he graciously excused himself, prompting Suzzy to escort him to the gate in a fond farewell gesture.

"Daddy, what do you think of Peter?" Suzzy asked, looking up at him with a warm smile from her seat.

"To be honest, Peter's a great guy - handsome and smart. But, for me, the fact that he's not part of our church is a major issue. I'd prefer someone from a good family within our congregation."

"Mom," Suzzy gazed tenderly at her mother.

"I agree with your father, Peter is a great guy with a wonderful character, but he's not a member of our church. And let's be real, there are plenty of amazing men within our congregation who might be interested in you," Mrs. Johnson said.

Suzzy's heart was shattered when her parents refused to accept Peter due to his humble background and different religious affiliation. Deeply in love with him, she found the pressure from her family was too much to bear. Despite her inner turmoil, she eventually moved on and found solace in Nathan's arms, a devoted member of her church. Nathan's love for Suzzy was evident in the sacrifices he made to ensure her happiness throughout their courtship.

Their decision to abstain from intimacy before marriage, in accordance with their church's teachings, demonstrated their commitment to their faith. After relocating from America, Nathan's seamless integration into the church community paved the way for his serendipitous encounter with Suzzy. Their love blossomed gradually, culminating in a blissful union solemnized within the sacred walls of their church.

The wedding ceremony was a joyous occasion, with the pastor's blessings sealing their union as a testament to their shared values and beliefs. Suzzy and Nathan began their new life together as a married couple, united by love and strengthen by their unwavering faith. From the trials of rejection and heartbreak, a beautiful love story emerged, anchored in faith and devotion.

On their wedding night, Suzzy eagerly anticipated intimate moments with her husband. She adorned herself in alluring attire, subtly attempting to capture Nathan's attention. However, Nathan seemed preoccupied with his phone, oblivious to Suzzy's seductive efforts.. Undeterred, she gently caressed his head and shoulders, hoping to draw him in. Nathan finally looked up, but instead of reciprocating her advances, he simply asked her to relax.

Suzzy felt disheartened by the lack of physical intimacy on their honeymoon. As the days passed without any romantic gestures from Nathan, doubts began to creep into her mind. The fourteen-day honeymoon was marked by a noticeable absence of affection between the newlyweds. Suzzy's anxiety grew, prompting her to confront Nathan about their fading connection.

In their conversation, Nathan revealed that his priorities in romantic relationships differed from Suzzy's. This confession struck Suzzy deeply, prompting her to reassess the foundation of their marriage.

"Then why did you even marry me?" Suzzy asked, her voice shaking with emotion.

"Come on, it's too early for this conversation."

Nathan told Suzzy to close the chapter on romance and lovemaking with him, as he was not interested or ready for such things with her. Suzzy was left speechless and weak. One day, Nathan went out and bought her toys to use on herself whenever she needed intimacy, or suggested she could go out and find someone else. He promised to pay her a large monthly allowance in exchange for her silence, as he couldn't bear the noise at home every morning. Nathan was very wealthy; his father, Mr. George Amu, was a prominent politician and entrepreneur who owned five successful companies in the country. Mr. Amu was also a close friend of Mr. Johnson, Suzzy's father, who served as his lawyer. The Amu family had helped the Johnsons' significantly, and Mr. Johnson was thrilled when Nathan proposed to Suzzy, believing he had found the best man for her.

A year had passed, and Suzzy found herself in a state of distress, burdened by the weight of her conscience to remain faithful. Despite the absence of physical intimacy in her marriage, she hesitated to seek solace elsewhere due to familial obligations and the mutual respect between their families. The palpable unhappiness did not go unnoticed by those around her, who inquired about her well-being. Yet, she steadfastly shielded her husband's reputation from any tarnish. Longing for a deeper connection, she wrestled with the temptation of seeking intimacy beyond the confines of her marriage, even though her husband had granted her permission.

The situation Suzzy found herself in was truly tormenting her emotional well-being. Devoid of any facade of fake smiles or pretense, Suzzy felt like she was merely existing, akin to a zombie wandering through life. The weight of the situation had slowly but surely been gnawing away at her, leaving her feeling drained and diminished. Her once-radiant and beautiful curvy figure was now fading, giving way to a more gaunt and frail appearance.

In times like these, the age-old adage that "a problem shared is a problem half solved" rings true. However, Suzzy knew all too well that not everyone is worthy of being entrusted with one's deepest struggles. It's essential to confide in someone who won't exploit your vulnerabilities or use your secrets against you for their own amusement. Trust is a fragile commodity, especially when one is grappling with inner turmoil.

Seeking solace in sharing her burden with a trusted confidant became a pressing need for Suzzy. The weight of her troubles seemed unbearable to carry alone, and opening up to someone trustworthy offered a glimmer of hope in the darkness that had enveloped her. The power of human connection and empathy cannot be overstated in moments of profound distress.

One quiet afternoon, after Nathan had finished his meal and was preparing to drift off into a brief slumber as was his custom, Suzzy casually mentioned that she was planning to visit a friend. With a sense of purpose, she exited the room, made her way to her sleek 2020 Range Rover Sport – a thoughtful birthday gift from Nathan – and drove off into the distance. The gentle tunes of country music filled the car, creating a soothing ambiance as she contemplated the conversation she was about to have with her trusted friend.

As she navigated the familiar streets, Suzzy's mind wandered back to the last time she had attempted to confide in Benedicta, only to swallow her words. This time, however, she was determined to share her innermost thoughts with Benedicta, a friend she had known since their university days, where their bond had deepened as roommates. Late-night chats and shared secrets had solidified their friendship, making Benedicta the perfect confidante.

Upon arriving at Benedicta's residence, Suzzy was warmly welcomed by the security personnel, who recognized her and promptly opened the gates. She parked carefully and made her way to Benedicta's front door, feeling a mix of nerves and anticipation. Benedicta, who had been abroad during Suzzy's wedding to Nathan, was visibly shocked as Suzzy began recounting her story. Her eyes widened in disbelief, and she struggled to find the right words to express her emotions.

As Suzzy poured her heart out, Benedicta's hands grew cold, and goosebumps appeared on her skin, a physical manifestation of her shock. Overwhelmed by the weight of Suzzy's words, Benedicta instinctively buried her face in her palms, taking a moment to process everything. She finally looked up, letting out a deep sigh.

"I had no idea things were this tough for you. I'm shocked that someone like Nathan could be so indifferent to someone as amazing as you. Have you thought about talking to your parents about what's going on? They need to know what you're going through. Keeping all this inside can really take a toll on you, Suzzy."

"If I tell my parents about this, it would be a total embarrassment for my husband. Plus, his dad has no idea about his real sexual orientation. If I spill the beans now, I know my parents will want me to divorce him, and then everyone will be asking questions about why our perfect marriage fell apart after just over a year. But honestly, keeping this secret is becoming too much to handle. On the other hand, if I don't tell my parents, I'll be stuck living a lie forever, and I'll never get to experience the happiness of being a mom."

"You remember Serwaa? Our old roommate who totally lost it when she found out her best friend was flirting with Peter, your ex. Yeah, that was crazy!"

Suzzy nodded.

"I want to share something with you because I trust you, and I know you can relate. Serwaa came to visit me last week and opened up about something personal. She told me she's bisexual." Suzzy's eyes snapped up, meeting Benedicta's gaze. "Yeah, Serwaa confided in me. She wants to tell her husband about her attraction to women, but she's not sure how to bring it up. She said her mom actually introduced her to all this when she was just 14! Can you believe it? After her parents split when she was 7, she lived with her mom until she got married at 28."

"When Serwaa was 14, her mom started getting really close to her, touching her in ways that felt weird at first, but eventually, she got used to it. By 16, they were basically sex partners, spending all day indoors doing stuff that wasn't normal. She stopped seeing her mom as her mom, more like a peer or something. She lost respect for her and pretty much everyone else. They'd fight like equals, then make up like lovers. Her grades suffered, but somehow she still managed to get good marks, probably because she was in a great school."

So, Serwaa was 24 when she met her husband, and she didn't sleep with him before they got married. Honestly, she wasn't really into guys, but there was something about him that was different. He was the first man she felt comfortable enough to open up to, so she decided to give him a chance. She'd been hiding her true feelings for a long time, but he brought out a side of her she hadn't explored before."

"So, her mom wasn't thrilled about her setting boundaries, but she was determined to prioritize her relationship with her husband and have a separate connection with her mom. By the time she was 27, she knew she needed to take a stand and create some distance. It wasn't easy, but she finally moved out of her mom's house, ready to start fresh and gain some independence. Her mom tried to win her back, but she held her ground until she felt ready for marriage. Eventually, her mom had to accept her decision and let her move on. Even after getting married, she still missed her mom sometimes and would visit her to catch up. But over time, their visits became less frequent, and it's been almost three years since they last saw each other."

Suzzy wiped away her tears, composed herself, and settled into her seat, becoming fully engrossed in the conversation. Benedicta continued…

"So, she found someone special - another woman - and they really connected. It was great for both of them, but she still loved her husband and didn't want to hurt him by getting a divorce. The problem was, she couldn't be honest with him about her feelings or who she really was. So, she came up with this idea to have a threesome with her husband and her girlfriend, who's also bi. That way, everyone gets what they want, right? But, it wasn't easy getting her husband on board with it, and now things have gotten pretty wild."

"She introduced this threesome to her husband, and now he seems to be more into her girlfriend than her! Whenever they're together, her husband is more focused on her friend than her. And it's not just that - her husband and her friend are getting closer and closer. She's realized she needs to end this threesome thing and focus on her relationships with her husband and her girlfriend separately. But, it's too late... her girlfriend is pregnant and wants to keep the baby. And here's the thing - her husband is the father, and she can't let that happen. Now, her girlfriend has become her enemy, and her husband has no idea what's going on. She wants to confess to him before her girlfriend does and try to separate them. She's going through a lot, and she's totally confused about what to do now..."

"Suzzy, honestly, it's better to be single than to go through all this drama. My advice is to tell your parents everything and let them handle it. Do you really want to protect some guy's reputation at the cost of your own happiness? Think about it - it's better to face some criticism and be free than to get praise and be stuck in a toxic situation forever. You're losing yourself in this marriage, Suzzy - your spark, your confidence, your beauty... it's all fading away. You look older than you are, while your husband seems to be aging backwards! That's not okay. You need to talk to your parents and get out of this marriage. Stop covering for someone who's hurting you emotionally. Please, go to your parents' place and tell them everything. Get out of this situation, Suzzy."

Suzzy's eyes brimmed with tears, which cascaded down her cheeks as she blinked away her sorrow. Benedicta approached her, offering solace, and Suzzy gratefully rested her head on Benedicta's shoulder before departing for her parents' house.

Suzzy parked her vehicle on the premises and proceeded directly to the living area, where Mr. and Mrs. Johnson were seated in the dining room, enjoying their early dinner at approximately 5:00 pm. Suzzy exchanged greetings with her parents and joined them at the dining table, although her mother offered her food, she lacked the desire to eat, appearing visibly discontent. Her parents observed her accelerated aging with concern, having previously inquired about it, to which she had dismissed their worries. They even thought that her deteriorating appearance might be attributed to a potential pregnancy, a suggestion she refuted. Her father shot her with a sorrowful glance. "Hey, if something's bothering you, please don't hesitate to tell us. We're your parents, and we're here for you.," Mr. Johnson expressed.

Suzzy let out a deep sigh and began recounting her harrowing tale, sparing no detail. She started from the night of their wedding and laid bare the truth to her parents, conveying the agony and torment she had endured. She expressed her yearning to break free from the confines of her marriage. Her parents were incredulous, with Mrs. Johnson still grappling with the revelations. The man they had deemed 'honorable' and the perfect match for their daughter had morphed into her tormentor, leaving them disillusioned with themselves as parents. They Provided solace to Suzzy and vowed to liberate her from her ordeal.

Two weeks later, the Johnson family's living room were filled with guests, including Mr. Johnson and his wife, Mr. George Amu and his wife, the church Pastor, and two church elders, Nathan and Suzzy. Mr. Johnson asked Suzzy to recount her story, leaving Nathan bewildered, as he was unaware of what she was about to share. Although his father had informed him about the meeting at Mr. Johnson's house, he had failed to ask if Suzzy had confided in her parents. As Suzzy commenced narrating her account, all eyes turned to Nathan, and discomfort settled in his mind. The air conditioning made him feel unusually warm, causing beads of sweat to form on his forehead. The revelation Suzzy made about him shocked Mr. George Amu and his wife, and the pastor and elders were equally taken aback. When he was given the chance to respond to Suzzy's accusations, Nathan acknowledged their validity. Mr. and Mrs. Amu were left speechless.

"I'm sad to say my daughter's going through a tough time, and honestly, I don't think she should stay in this marriage. Her husband's suggestion that she sleep with other men whenever she wants physical affection is just outrageous - it's completely disrespectful to her. And let's be real, Nathan clearly doesn't care about her, so there's no reason for them to keep pretending to be married. I think it's time to face facts and end this marriage once and for all," Mr. Johnson said, his voice firm and resolute.

Mr. Amu had little to say, expressing his disappointment as he acquiesced to the termination of the marriage. He apologized to the Johnson family for the disgrace caused by his son's action. The pastor and elders also remained silent, concurring with both families on the dissolution of the marital union.

After three days, the divorce papers were signed, and Suzzy returned to her parents' home. Mr. and Mrs. Johnson acknowledged their mistakes; first, they had dictated Mawu's future path, leading to her departure, and second, they had arranged Suzzy's marriage, nearly losing her as well. They pledged to refrain from meddling in their children's pursuit of happiness, opting instead to serve as trusted advisors when needed.

CHAPTER TEN

AGBOGBLOSHIE FIRE OUTBREAK

The Agbogbloshie market, situated in the bustling heart of Accra, was a vibrant hub of commerce where buyers and sellers from various regions across the country converged daily. It was more than just a market; it was a thriving ecosystem where the pulse of trade and livelihoods beat strongly. Vendors came far and wide, from the lush landscapes of the Central and Eastern regions to the remote corners of the Oti and Volta regions, to showcase their diverse array of goods.

This market was more than just a place to buy and sell; it was a vibrant melting pot of cultures, flavors, and stories. The aroma of freshly harvested vegetables blended with the sizzle of meats on grills, creating a sensory symphony that drew food enthusiasts from far and wide. For Accra's top restaurants, Agbogbloshie market was a lifeline, providing a steady supply of fresh produce that showcase their menus and delighted the palates of their patrons.

Amidst the bustling commerce, the market also shone as a beacon of hope for many struggling individuals. Unemployed youth and parents found opportunities in the chaos, either by traveling to rural villages to source goods for sale or by setting up small stalls within the market. The sight of young girls, some barely out of childhood, carrying infants on their backs as they navigated the crowded alleys, was a poignant reminder of the hardships faced by many.

Despite the vibrancy and energy that characterized the market, a darker side lurked beneath the surface. The makeshift tents that served as temporary shelters for weary vendors and the vulnerable, the prevalence of sexual violence against women, and the harsh realities faced by truck pushers and hawkers who toiled tirelessly painted a stark contrast to the market's lively facade.

In the midst of this dynamic marketplace, where dreams were born and shattered in equal measure, the Agbogbloshie market stood as a powerful testament to the resilience and tenacity of the human spirit. It was a place where fortunes were made and lost, and where the echoes of laughter and the shadows of despair were intricately intertwined in a complex tapestry of life.

Mawu and Adjei, two hardworking individuals, lived in a humble kiosk within the bustling market, diligently paying their monthly rent of 50 Ghana cedis. As truck pushers and loaders, they worked long hours under the scorching sun, earning a modest daily income of 30 to 50 Ghana cedis. The toil and sweat required to make a living in the market were not to be underestimated, as every penny had to be earned through manual labor.

Mawu and Adjei's daily routine involved assisting drivers in unloading goods from trucks and then loading them onto their own makeshift wooden truck for transportation to their designated destinations. In exchange for their labor, they earned their hard-earned wages. Despite their meager earnings, they practiced frugality by eating only one meal a day and diligently saving the remainder of their money in a "susu" account.

In Ghana, "susu" collectors, a traditional form of financial intermediary, provided a secure means for market individuals to save money and access limited credit. This method of saving was widely adopted by many market-goers due to its reliability and accessibility.

However, not everyone in the market engaged in honest work like Mawu and Adjei. The market had a darker side, with various ghettos harboring individuals involved in social vices. These included teenage girls who turned to prostitution to survive, as well as men and women who resorted to drug peddling. The harsh reality of their existence forced them into a cycle of dependency on illicit activities.

Prostitutes in the market could earn between 20 to 30 Ghana cedis a day, depending on the number of clients and market conditions. However, some resorted to substance abuse to cope with their circumstances, leading to addiction and a deteriorating physical appearance. The toll of their lifestyle was evident in their neglect of personal hygiene, resulting in health issues and a subsequent decline in clientele.

The market, a microcosm of society, showcased both the resilience of individuals like Mawu and Adjei and the harsh realities faced by those trapped in cycles of poverty and vice. Amidst the hustle and bustle of daily life, each person navigated their own path, striving to make ends meet in a challenging and unforgiving environment.

Mabel and her partner, Solo, were involved in the distribution of illicit substances, primarily dealing in marijuana, morphine, and cocaine as their main source of income. Their routine involved procuring narcotics from a notorious drug lord in the ghetto, who would give them a specific quantity to sell and include a commission. They would then navigate the market, catering to their established clientele, mostly individuals seeking stimulants to sustain prolonged physical labor, such as truck off-loaders and pushers. While Mabel smoked cigarettes and consuming alcohol, Solo preferred marijuana, occasionally mixing it with a small amount of morphine and alcohol. As they traversed the streets, offering their merchandise, their daughter Lina was always with them, securely carried on Mabel's back regardless of the weather. Engaging in such a perilous trade within the ghetto carried severe risks, as a single misstep could have fatal consequences.

At 2 a.m. on Wednesday, chaos engulfed the market as a raging fire swept through the area. Smoke billowed through the air, flames danced wildly, and a sense of urgency gripped the scene. People frantically fled their homes, the sound of screams and shouts echoing through the night. Amidst the pandemonium, brave souls attempted to douse the inferno, but it raged on relentlessly. The arrival of the fire service remained uncertain, casting doubt on whether salvation would come in time. This tragic event marked the fourth market fire of the year, each previous incident ending in devastation before help could arrive. Structures crumbled, livelihoods vanished in the flames, and the community stood helpless as the fire consumed everything in its path. Despite the valiant efforts of those nearby, the uncontrollable blaze continued its destructive path, leaving a trail of destruction and despair in its wake.

It was 5:00 a.m. when the national fire service finally arrived with their tanker, but the blaze had already decimated everything in its path. The onlookers and the general public were outraged by the fire service personnel's tardiness. To make matters worse, their tanker was empty, devoid of water upon arrival, prompting the inevitable question, "What was the point of their delayed response?"

A sense of dysfunction pervaded the country as the root cause of the fire outbreak remained a mystery. The national fire service had yet to launch an investigation, leaving the public to fill the void with speculation. Politicization of the incident began to spread, with some speculating that the opposition party orchestrated the market infernos to undermine the government's credibility. Others insinuated that the government itself orchestrated the fires to shift blame onto the opposition party and sway voters' opinions, particularly with elections on the horizon.

At approximately 8:00 a.m., the national fire service rescue team begun their somber task of searching for and locating individuals who had perished in the fire tragedy. The incident had resulted in a devastating number of casualties and fatalities. The scene was heart-wrenching as individuals who had traveled from various villages to the city were now laid to rest in a communal grave. Those who had managed to survive bore visible scars, with burns on their faces and other parts of their bodies serving as a poignant remainder of the tragedy.

The vice president visited the site to survey the damage and inspect the casualties, pledging to provide a substantial sum of money to individuals who suffered property loss or injuries in the fire incident. The aim was to help them rebuild their lives, but some viewed this as mere political rhetoric that would never materialize. Others remained hopeful of receiving the promised funds, especially since it was an election year. "Is this just a ploy to evoke sympathy from us, only to later offer empty consolation?" one of the victims wondered quietly.

Mawu's disappearance had left Adjei and their friends in a state of deep distress. The first aid team had tended to Adjei's injury, carefully bandaging his head and arm, which had been cut and broken in the chaos. The tragedy had claimed the lives of six of their friends from the ghetto, a devastating loss. Adjei vividly remembered the heartbreaking moment when he saw the rescue team solemnly carrying Amartey's lifeless body away in a sack, tears streaming down his face as he struggled to come to terms with the loss.

Amartey, a resident of the market where he lived with his mother, Auntie Ayorkor, played a significant role in the lives of Adjei and Mawu. Whenever they were without money for food, they would often seek solace in Auntie Ayorkor's generosity; she never hesitated to provide them with kenkey and fish, trusting they would repay her. Auntie Ayorkor, renowned for her delicious Ga kenkey and fried fish sold in the market, miraculously survived the fire that claimed the life of her beloved son, Amartey.

The bond between Mawu, Adjei, and their friends was rooted in camaraderie, mutual support, and reliance on each other during times of need. The tragic loss of Amartey was a stark reminder of life's fragility and the unpredictability of fate. Despite the devastation, the memories of their departed friends would remain forever etched in their hearts, serving as a poignant reminder of the preciousness of every shared moment.

Adjei was in anguish, tears streaming uncontrollably down his cheeks. His eyes darted frantically in every direction, searching for any sign of Mawu. Before the inferno engulfed their surroundings that fateful night, Mawu had mentioned she was heading towards the women's lavatory, situated approximately twenty meters away from their kiosk. Five minutes had elapsed when the flames erupted. Rushing to the ladies' toilet, Adjei found it empty, prompting a swift return to their kiosk, only to witness it consumed by the raging fire. A sharp object grazed his head, propelling him to flee for safety. "Mawu can't be trapped in that inferno... I won't let myself think that. She's probably out there searching for me right now. I have to find her.," he reassured himself, steadfastly refusing to entertain pessimistic thoughts.

The rescue team extricated others from the scene, who were unconscious and required prompt transfer to the hospital for urgent medical attention. Mawu, however, was conspicuously absent. Adjei spotted Solo and quickly approached him.

"Hey, did you see Mawu anywhere? And what about Mabel and Lina? Are they around?"

"I haven't seen Mawu... And, bro, I've got some bad news. Mabel and Lina didn't make it. I got there too late, and... I couldn't save them." Solo's words faltered as tears welled in his eyes and cascaded down his cheeks, overcome with emotion, he wept.

The destitute mother and her daughter tragically perished in a raging inferno. A young pregnant woman, unjustly expelled from her parents' home, met a tragic demise.

CHAPTER ELEVEN

MAWU'S DISAPPEARANCE

A month had passed since the tragic incident at Agbogbloshie, yet Adjei's emotional and mental wounds still lingered. Physically, he had recovered from his broken arm, but the trauma remained. His best friend and sister, Mawu was still missing, her whereabouts unknown. Despite his tireless efforts to gather information from acquaintances, no one seemed to know anything about her fate. The loss of five friends, including Mabel and Lina, in the devastating fire had left him heartbroken. The haunting image of the young mother and her daughter, reduced to ashes with only their skulls and charred flesh remaining, refused to leave his mind. Adjei struggled to comprehend the cruelty of parents who would condemn their daughter to such a fate for a teenage pregnancy, hiding behind the guise of religion while perpetuating unspeakable acts. He grappled with the hypocrisy, grieving for Mabel and her innocent child, lost to the senseless tragedy.

Adjei incessantly inquired of acquaintances about Mawu's whereabouts. His recent inability to work due to a fractured arm had left him in financial distress. Despite experiencing a loss of appetite in the weeks following Mawu's disappearance, Adjei found himself without even a penny to spare, not even for the restroom. Auntie Ayorkor, preoccupied with mourning her son, was unavailable to sell her food, denying Adjei the opportunity to obtain food on credit. However, his friends offered him solace by inviting him to share their evening meals, leaving the daytime hours for fasting, a practice he was familiar with. His thoughts were consumed by the search for Mawu and the burning question of her location. Despite scouring the market and the charred remnants for any trace that might lead him to Mawu, his efforts were in vain. Refusing to entertain the possibility that Mawu had perished in the fire, Adjei clung to his unwavering optimism. Seating himself on a large rock nestled amidst the scorched trees, he gazed around in hopeful anticipation of Mawu's return. A glimmer of hope ignited within him as he spotted a young woman approaching, prompting him to rise eagerly and advance towards her, whispering in elation, "Thank the heavens, I have found Mawu." Upon reaching the lady, however, his hopes were dashed as he realized his mind had played a cruel trick on him.

The Agbogbloshie market's functionality had significantly declined, rendering it obsolete for trading activities. The Accra Metropolitan Assembly (AMA) issued a cautionary directive, urging the public to refrain from engaging in any business at the Agbogbloshie market until the National Fire Service completed its investigation and deemed the area safe and conducive for commercial operations. Approximately five months prior, Agbogbloshie market users staged a demonstration in response to the regional minister's proposal to relocate them to facilitate estate development on the market premises. Suspicions arose among the populace, who speculated that the government and the minister might have had prior knowledge related to the fire incident. The awaited outcome of the National Fire Service's investigation was eagerly anticipated, despite widespread skepticism towards state institutions, fueled by the perceptions of governmental influence over their operations.

Adabraka market stood as a prominent trading hub in Accra, situated approximately eight hundred meters from the bustling Agbogbloshie market. Over time, it had evolved into a bustling center of commerce, attracting a significant influx of vendors and customers who had previously frequented Agbogbloshie. Adjei, driven by the necessity to sustain himself, ventured into the Adabraka market in search of employment opportunities. Despite lacking the proper tools such as a head pan or wheelbarrow, to transport goods, his determination led him to scour the market for any available work. Having gone without food the previous evening and morning, he felt a slight dizziness, yet his dire circumstances compelled him to seek employment. By chance, he encountered a truck laden with yams at the eastern section of the market and promptly approached the driver. Pleading for the opportunity to assist in unloading the cargo in exchange for a meager sum to alleviate his hunger, Adjei's sincerity resonated with the driver, who granted his request. With unwavering diligence, he swiftly embarked on unloading the goods, impressing the driver with his industriousness. Grateful for the compensation he received, Adjei expressed his heartfelt appreciation to the driver for the unexpected generosity.

As evening settled in, a dusky hue cast over Adjei's new surroundings. The recent market fire had left him and Mawu without their kiosk, forcing Adjei to spend his nights in the open space within the lorry station. Among the various individuals who also sought refuge there, a makeshift community formed under the night sky, comprising both males and females.

Adjei utilized the public bathroom facilities at the lorry station, despite the nominal fee required for each use, which limited him to bathing only once a day. After completing his evening routine of bathing and dinner, he felt a sense of unease. Although he had some funds saved with the susu collector, he refrained from withdrawing them until he could reunite with Mawu. However, Mawu's absence weighed heavily on Adjei's mind, prompting him to embark on a nocturnal quest through the surrounding ghettos in search of her.

With a sense of determination, Adjei combed through the dimly lit alleys and bustling streets, hoping to catch a glimpse of Mawu amidst the shadows. His search took him to unexpected corners of the neighborhood, as he left no stone unturned in his pursuit. However, despite his tireless efforts, the night yielded no sign of Mawu. Disheartened, Adjei returned to the lorry station, seeking respite before the early morning departure to the market at dawn.

At precisely 3:30 a.m., Adjei awoke, refreshed his face with sachet water, and thoroughly gargled. Placing a traditional chewing stick in his mouth, he set out for the market, intending to arrive by 4:00 a.m. to assist in unloading another truck of yams. The driver had explicitly instructed him to be punctual. The journey from the lorry station to the market typically took him approximately 25 minutes. Remarkably, he arrived 8 minutes ahead of the truck's arrival. Upon spotting him, the driver greeted him warmly and shut off the engine. "How are you, my boy?" the driver inquired. "I am well, boss," Adjei responded with a smile. Two other men joined him by the truck, deftly catching and meticulously arranging the yams as they were tossed down. By

6:20 a.m., they successfully completed the task of unloading and organizing the yams, and Adjei received his compensation. Eager to locate Mawu, he decided to explore the market. After a brief search, he opted to visit the hospitals where the injured had been taken, hoping to gather any potential information about Mawu's whereabouts.

He strolled approximately three hundred meters from the marketplace to the Adabraka polyclinic, braving the scorching afternoon sun. He chose not to board a "trotro," hoping to chance upon Mawu on his way elsewhere. Upon reaching the polyclinic, he inquired with two nurses, who searched through their records but could not locate Mawu's name. Undeterred by his disappointment, he remained optimistic and decided to trek to Iran Hospital, situated about three hundred meters away from the Adabraka polyclinic. Arriving promptly at 2:00 pm, he approached the receptionist and was directed to the office of a senior nurse. After describing Mawu to her, he was once again met with disappointment. The nurse recommended trying his luck at Ridge Hospital, six hundred meters away from Iran Hospital. Despite his fatigue, he clung to hope, and fortunately, the sun's intensity had subsided. Making his way to Ridge Hospital, he had the opportunity to converse with a nurse who kindly offered him a seat while reviewing the list of patients admitted that day. After calling Adjei to the reception counter, she informed him that there was no record of a patient named Mawu.

"Please, were you working that day?" Adjei asked, hesitating to leave without any clue about Mawu's fate.

"Yeah, I was working that day with my colleague, who's actually here right now. Let me just grab her for a sec," she said, stepping away for a moment before returning with another nurse.

"Hi, I'm Adjei. I think my sister might have been brought here. Do you remember a girl with cornrows, wearing a yellow shirt with flowers and a wine-colored skirt? She's got chocolate skin, about 157 centimeters tall, and has hairy arms and legs. That's my sister, Mawu. Do you recognize her?" Adjei meticulously detailed Mawu's appearance.

"Oh, Afi! That's the one," the nurse said to her colleague. "She's the lady I was telling you about who took off without leaving any contact info of her family." Turning to Adjei, she explained, "Yes, she was here, but she disappeared last Monday. She refused to give us any details about her relatives.."

"Afi's her name too, but we call her Mawu at home. Thank you so much for telling me this! I'm such a relief to know my sister is alive." Adjei gave them a radiant smile . After expressing his gratitude, he left the hospital with a sense of elation, his heart brimming with joy. Overwhelmed with happiness, he felt as though he had won the lottery. On his way home, he indulged in his favorite meal: crispy yam accompanied by fried octopus sprinkled with fiery chili pepper. It was a day filled with jubilation, prompting him to pamper himself as he eagerly anticipated reuniting with Mawu. Upon reaching the lorry station where he had been lodging, he discreetly retrieved a black polythene bag hidden behind a lotto kiosk. Carefully untying the bag, he extracted his sponge and soap before heading to the communal bathing area.

It was around 8:00 pm, and after finishing his meal, he ventured out into the streets once more to search for Mawu. Throughout the night, he meticulously scoured the various shops and lorry stations, inquiring about Mawu's whereabouts, but luck eluded him. Despite this setback, he found solace in the nurses' confirmation that Mawu was indeed alive, which reassured him that their reunion was imminent. With this comforting thought, he returned to the lorry station and fell asleep for the night.

It was 4 o'clock in the early hours of the morning. The bus conductors had commenced tidying their bus seats, while the drivers inspected the engine oils and checked for any potential faults in the vehicles before loading passengers. Adjei, already awake and prepared to depart for the market, stood in silence for a moment, offering a quiet prayer to the divine, seeking a favorable day ahead.

Arriving at the market around 4:30 am, Adjei found that the truck was not there that day. So, he decided to rent a wheelbarrow within the market premises to transport people's goods for a fee. The day looked promising as he attracted more clients seeking his services to carry their merchandise to the roadside. While loading a woman's provisions onto the wheelbarrow, he suddenly heard his name being called. He glanced over and recognized Peter, then walked over to approach him.

"Adjei, I just hear for news say the money wey Vice President promise give to the people wey suffer go dey share am dis morning for 10:00am for Central Police Station!" Peter gasped, having rushed to Adjei to relay the news as soon as he heard it.

"Thank God oh! Na almost 8 o'clock, make we hustle small, so we go fit commot for 9 o'clock. Di trek from here go Central

Police Station no go take pass 30 minutes." Adjei's smile began to fade.

"Bro, wetin dey worry you? Everything okay?" Peter became apprehensive.

"I just dey think of Mawu, if she dey here, we for go collect dis money together."

"I understand you, bro, but calm down. Who know, maybe we go meet am for there."

Adjei grinned and gently patted Peter on the shoulder, "Your words dey sweet me, bro!" he said. "Make dem come true as you don see am!." He added, "I go meet you by 9:00am, no be late" With that, Peter bid farewell, and Adjei resumed his tasks.

Adjei and Peter arrived at the central police station premises at 9:25 am precisely. A crowd had already gathered, eagerly awaiting the distribution of their funds. Adjei scanned the crowd intently, searching for Mawu, although he had a hunch that she was present, he couldn't be certain. About five minutes after their arrival, a gentleman in his fifties, adorned in traditional African attire and holding a stack of documents, called for everyone's attention.

"Alright everyone, we've got a list here of people affected by the recent fire. I'll be calling out names one by one. When you hear your name, please come forward and head to the charge room to pick up an envelope with some financial assistance. Once you've got your envelope, please exit the premises. Got it?"

They all replied affirmatively, and he began listing the names. Each person who entered to receive an envelope left with a smile. When Peter's name was called, he collected his envelope and waited patiently for Adjei. After several more names were called, Adjei finally heard his own and went inside to retrieve his envelope. Upon exiting the building, just as he was about to leave through the gate, a voice called out, "Afi Mawu!" Adjei quickly turned towards the speaker and spotted someone resembling Mawu entering the room. As he drew closer, his heart racing with anticipation, Mawu emerged. With a cry of joy, Adjei called out to Mawu, who turned, ran towards him, and embraced him tightly. Tears of happiness streamed down their faces as they reunited. As they exited the premises, they encountered Peter, overjoyed to see Mawu return unharmed.

They discovered a serene spot and settled down to talk. Adjei shared with Mawu the sad news of their friends' passing, including Amartey, Mabel, and her daughter. Mawu was overcome with sorrow, bowing her head and releasing a deep sigh.

"Adjei, remember that evening when I said I was going to the ladies' room? I saw Solo rushing off in the distance, and I didn't want to bother him, so I just kept going. But then I saw this huge cloud of smoke and heard crackling and popping noises coming from Mabel's area. I ran towards it, and oh my god, her kiosk and a few others were on fire! I could hear Lina crying and Mabel begging for help. I tried to put out the flames with some sand, but it was no use. The fire was spreading fast, and I was worried about you. I didn't know what to do - go back to our kiosk to make sure you were okay or try to help Mabel and her daughter. Next thing I knew, I was waking up in the hospital, totally confused. I was scared they'd call my parents, so I took off. Now I'm living and working at the Mallam Atta market, searching for you everywhere. I've been walking around for days, hoping to run into you."

CHAPTER TWELVE

A SEARCH FOR MAWU

Mrs. Johnson's unease was palpable, a subtle yet undeniable sense of something amiss lingering in the air around her. Despite her best efforts, she couldn't pinpoint the source of her discomfort, knowing only that it was there, lurking just beyond her grasp. Her heartbeat seemed slightly off-rhythm, a subtle irregularity that set her on edge. As she tentatively touched her skin, a chill ran through her, signaling that this was no ordinary malaise.

Then, a sudden gust of warm wind swept past her, causing her to startle and rise to her feet, with a cry escaping her lips: "Mawu!" It had been precisely four long years since Mawu had departed from their home, leaving behind a void that seemed to grow with each passing day. Despite Mawu's assurance to her parents four years ago that she would be safe and well, Mrs. Johnson couldn't shake off the worry that gnawed at her heart.

Night after night, she found herself drawn to Mawu's empty room, where tears mingled with fervent prayers for her daughter's protection and swift return. Mrs. Johnson knew that the bond between a mother and child was unbreakable and enduring, a love that transcended time and distance. Regret weighed heavily on her as she reflected on her perceived lack of support for Mawu's chosen path, blaming herself for the fracture that had driven Mawu away.

In the midst of her turmoil, a familiar voice broke through her thoughts. "Mom, I heard you call out for Mawu. Is everything okay?" Suzzy asked, her voice laced with concern.

Following her divorce from Nathan, Suzzy found herself in a new chapter of her life. Despite the unexpected turn of events, she embraced the opportunity to reconnect with her parents and seek solace in their comforting presence. Moving back under their roof allowed her to rediscover a sense of security and familiarity she had been missing. This period of healing and self-discovery enabled Suzzy to gradually regain her confidence and inner strength. Throughout this journey, Mrs. Johnson played a pivotal role in Suzzy's emotional and psychological recovery.

"I just want to see my daughter again... I've been longing to lay eyes on Mawu for four years now, and it's been eating away at me. How can I even sleep at night when I don't know where she is or if she's okay? Is she safe? Is she eating well? It's like my mind is constantly racing with worst-case scenarios. I just can't shake this feeling that something's wrong, that she's not doing alright," Mrs. Johnson said, tears streaming down her face.

"Mom, I know Mawu's a strong woman who promised to come back home once she's achieved her goals, but it's really weird that we haven't heard from her in four years. I've tried reaching out to her friends and searching for her in Accra, but I've had no luck. It's like she vanished into thin air. I'm at a loss for where to even start looking for her when we decide to search for her." Suzzy said, helping her mother settle onto the sofa.

"We're going to find Mawu, Suzzy. I just know it. I don't know where we'll start or where it'll take us, but I trust that God will lead the way. We'll figure it out as we go. I have to find my daughter, no matter what it takes."

The next day, Mrs. Johnson and Suzzy set out in search of Mawu. Although they were unsure where to commence, Mrs. Johnson remained steadfast in her belief that the Holy Spirit would guide them. She carefully followed the inner voice that directed her on which routes to take and turns to make. Sitting beside her mother in the front seat, Suzzy gazed out the side window, scanning the surroundings for any sign of her sister's presence. A solemn atmosphere filled the car as Mrs. Johnson navigated the roads. Noticing the somber expression on her mother's face, Suzzy felt compelled to start a conversation, sensing her mother's preoccupation with thoughts.

"'ll never forget the time my car broke down and I had to hop on a Trotro to make a meeting. So, I'm on the ride, and this guy starts beefing with the conductor over the fare. They get into this intense argument, and the conductor's like, 'Pay up or get out!' The guy finally pays, but I can tell he's still fuming. Then, when he gets off, he suddenly smacks the conductor! I mean, it was loud, and the conductor was visibly shaken. But you know what? Everyone else in the Trotro just burst out laughing. That's when I realized, Trotro rides can be wild and unpredictable, but also kinda hilarious."

Suzzy noticed the radiant smiles adorning her mother's face, which filled her with joy. She was determined to alleviate her mother's incessant worrying.

Uncertainty loomed over the quest for Mawu's whereabouts, but Suzzy remained resolute, drawing strength from her mother's unwavering faith and reliance on divine guidance.

"I had this crazy experience on a Trotro during my university days. There was this guy on board selling some herbal remedy for hemorrhoids, but nobody was paying attention. So, he starts cracking jokes to get our attention. He tells this hilarious story about a church crusade where someone prophesied, he'd walk - and he's thinking, 'Yeah, right, I've got no car.' But then he realizes his wallet's gone, and he's got no choice but to walk home!" Mrs. Johnson said, and they laughed so hard that it was infectious.

"He would've ended up walking all the way from Kotobabi to Ablekuma!" Suzzy said with a chuckle.

"I had an interesting encounter at the Mallam Atta market last week. I was about to leave after shopping for some household essentials when a gentleman approached me. He asked for a minute, and I agreed, curious about what he wanted. He told me about his job as a head porter and how he'd helped an elderly woman carry her cassava across the road. But then, disaster struck - a motorcyclist crashed into him, and he fell, injuring his hand. The rider took off without helping, but a kind taxi driver tried to chase him down. Unfortunately, the rider got away. The poor guy needed GHc650 for treatment, but he couldn't afford it. I was surprised he spoke English so well! I asked more questions, and we chatted - his name is Mawutor. I felt bad for him, so I gave him GHc1000 for his medical bills and promised to visit him at the market soon. Let's stop by and see how he's doing, okay?"

"Okay mom," Suzzy agreed.

They arrived at the marketplace and asked one of the female "head potters" to inquire about Mawutor. The lady instructed them to be patient while she went to fetch Mawutor.

Mawutor arrived with his hand wrapped in a bandage.

"Good morning maa," Mawutor greeted with a radiant smile.

"Hey, you're looking good! I hope your treatment went well. I was in the area and thought I'd drop by to see how you're doing. I hope you are not working with that hand bandaged up like that?"

"Yeah, maa, I'm doing great, thanks for asking! Thanks so much for your help, it really made a big difference - the treatment went really well and I'm feeling awesome now. Don't worry, I'm not using my hand for work or anything, I was just chillin' under the tent when she came to get me," Mawutor said with a smile.

"Awesome, I'm so glad to hear you're doing well! I should get going, but I'll definitely stop by again soon. By the way, this is my daughter Suzzy - say hi!"

"Good morning Suzzy, nice to meet you," Mawutor smiled.

"Good morning Mawutor, nice to meet you too," Suzzy reciprocated with a warm smile.

"Okay, we should get going. Take care of yourself, Mawutor," Mrs. Johnson said, pressing some money into his hand. "Thank you so much, ma'am!" Mawutor exclaimed, his eyes widening in gratitude.

Just as Suzzy was about to open the front door, she paused and turned around. "Mawutor!" she called out, and he promptly approached her. She rummaged her handbag, pulled out her phone, and showed Mawutor a photograph.

"Kindly take a look at this photo and tell me if you've seen this person around here or anywhere else? I'd really appreciate your help in identifying her."

Mawutor gazed intently at the image, striving to recollect the identity of the person captured within it.

"She looks really familiar. I'm sure I've seen her around here before. Didn't she used to be one of the head potters? I thought she left a couple of weeks ago."

"Do you remember her name?" Mrs. Johnson asked.

"Yes maa, her name is Mawu."

Suzzy and Mrs. Johnson gazed at each other in astonishment.

"Yes, she's the one! Did she tell you where she was going or where she lives?" Mrs. Johnson asked, eager for any details.

"She told me she was a head potter at Agbogbloshie market before the fire. And she'd often spend her nights right there," Mawutor said, pointing to the shop behind them. "She'd hang out with the other girls in front of that store every evening after work."

"Thanks so much, Mawutor! I really appreciate your help," Suzzy said with a smile before turning to leave. "Take care, bye!"

Suzzy and her mother sat in the car and drove off. Overcome with emotion, they headed back home, unable to continue the search due to the tears in their eyes and the heavy burden in their hearts.

CHAPTER THIRTEEN

DISAPPOINTING EXPERIENCE

Mawu and Adjei were now working together at the Adabraka market, having purchased two new wheelbarrows with part of the funds from the vice president's pledge. They had wisely saved the remainder. With a new kiosk secured within the market, they had a place to rest and sleep. Since Sundays were observed as holidays across the various markets in Accra, with many attending church or simply relaxing, Mawu and Adjei sat on a sturdy wooden bench in their new surroundings. They were beneath a majestic mango tree that stood in front of their recently acquired kiosk.

"Growing up, I knew life wasn't easy, but I had no idea just how tough it could be. My dad was a big part of that - he was irresponsible and sometimes even cruel. I swore I wouldn't be like him, but for a while, I thought all men were the same. That was until I saw our neighbor, Uncle Norbert, apologize to his wife for messing up. It was a wake-up call.

"My dad would beat my mom whenever she confronted him about his cheating. He'd claim we didn't have enough money, but then he'd go spend it on other women at the bar. Meanwhile, my mom worked hard selling fried yam and fish on the street. We'd start prepping at 9 am and be done by 11 am. Then, we'd set up our displays and hit the streets - my mom with one, me with the other. She promised to get me back in school the next month..."

"So, how old were you when you started helping your mom vend on the streets? And did your dad even bother coming home for meals, or was he too busy eating out with other women?" Mawu asked, curiosity getting the better of her.

"I was just 11 years old when I started selling on the streets with my mom, two years before she passed away. My dad was already gone, emotionally and financially. He was too busy with another woman, Auntie Agatha, to care about us. He'd spend nights at her place, taking care of her kids like they were his own, but ignoring me like I didn't exist. I even wondered if he was really my dad, that's how little he cared. He showed no love, no concern, nothing. He was there physically, but I felt like I didn't have a father at all." He paused, choking back tears, and continued...

"One Tuesday morning, around 4:30 am, my mom told me she was heading to the market to buy a bunch of yams for the week. She usually got back by 8 am, but when it hit 9 am, then 10 am, and she still wasn't back, I started getting worried. I was sitting at the entrance of our house, waiting for her, when I saw my dad coming out of Auntie Agatha's place. I ran up to him and asked him to please call my mom to make sure she was okay, but he just brushed me off, saying he had no credit on his phone. He didn't even ask if I was doing alright or offer to help - he just walked away like he didn't care."

"By noon, my mom still wasn't back, and I was getting really worried. That's when Maame Adoley, our co-tenant, came to the door in tears. She looked at me with such sadness in her eyes, and I had no idea what was wrong. 'Your mother has passed away,' she whispered, and my heart just stopped. I felt a chill run down my spine, and I couldn't process what she was saying. I sat down, feeling numb, as she told me my mom had been in a car accident. I couldn't believe it. I ran to Auntie Agatha's house to tell my dad, but all he said was, 'So what should I do...' Like, what kind of response is that? He didn't even seem to care."

"That's just wicked! How can a father be so callous towards his own child? If he had problems with your mom, that's one thing, but to take it out on you? That's just wrong. Some people have no shame, no empathy... it's shocking. Is your dad still alive?" Mawu exclaimed, her indignation palpable.

"Yeah, he's probably still out there, living his life. But honestly, it's been so long since we last crossed paths, it feels like a lifetime ago. Sometimes I question the universe, wondering why people like him get to cause so much pain to kind-hearted people like my mom. It just doesn't make sense."

"I think marriage should be more like a business deal. You enter into a two-year contract, and if it's not working out, you can just walk away. No fuss, no muss. It's like a trial period - if you like it, you can renew, but if not, you can move on."

"I've got your back, Mawu! I won't let anyone mess with you. When you're ready to settle down, I'll be there to vet the guy and make sure he's worthy of you," Adjei said, smiling protectively.

"Aww, thank you so much, Adjei! You're so much like Frank, it's uncanny. I see so much of him in you, and it warms my heart. I'm really grateful for your love and support - it means everything to me. We're in this together, and I know we'll face whatever life throws our way, side by side."

"Mawu, you know? let's get serious about your music career. We've come a long way, worked hard, and saved some cash. It's time to take it to the next level! Let's start looking for opportunities, ditch the market, and find producers who can actually help us. I know it won't be easy, but we got to keep pushing and hope to find someone who's legit and wants to do business, not just hit on you. We can't just keep grinding without a plan and expect things to magically get better. We need to make a move, Mawu! With your three singles, we can start approaching radio stations and see if they'll play your stuff. Yeah, there might be some fees, but we can try to negotiate a decent price."

"I'm so grateful to have a brother like you! Your support and selflessness always blow me away. We've saved up a good amount, and now it's time for you also to focus on your education. As my manager, you'll be handling contracts and legal stuff, so you need to be solid on English and talent management basics. I'm counting on you to be my rock, so please make sure you're prepared. I know I can trust you to get this done," Mawu said with a warm smile.

"I get it, but let's prioritize - your development comes first. I've been thinking, and with the TV3 mentor auditions coming up, we should totally go for it! I believe in you so much, and I know you'll crush it. Even if you don't win, the exposure to top managers and record labels will be huge for your career. I'm convinced this mentorship will be a game-changer for you. Let's do this, Mawu - let's take this journey together!"

"You know I can't go public with my identity right now because of family issues, right?"

"Exactly! That's why I'm your manager - to handle all the behind-the-scenes stuff. Don't worry, I've got a solution for the identity thing. We'll get you a mask to wear on stage, and it'll be your trademark, your signature look!" Adjei exclaimed, offering Mawu a high-five.

"Manager one!" Mawu hailed Adjei.

TV3 Mentor was a renowned Ghanaian music reality show that aimed to discover and nurture emerging music talents in the country. The show, which aired on TV3, a well-established Ghanaian television network, had successfully completed several seasons. The format typically featured a competition series of performances, eliminations, and mentorship from experienced music professionals. Aspiring musicians navigated these challenging stages, vying for the ultimate prize: a coveted recording contract and other lucrative rewards designed to launch the winner's music career.

Over the years, TV3 Mentor has played a pivotal role in launching the careers of many accomplished Ghanaian musicians, solidifying its status as a beloved and highly anticipated program in Ghana's thriving music scene. The show's auditions were strategically held in various regions on different dates to facilitate widespread participation. The journey began with the initial audition in Kumasi, situated in the culturally rich Ashanti region. Next, aspiring talents showcased their skills in Takoradi, a coastal gem in the Western region, before concluding with the final audition at the prestigious TV3 premises in Accra, the vibrant capital of the Greater Accra region.

The meticulous planning and execution of these auditions added an extra layer of excitement and anticipation, while also allowing for a diverse pool of talents to be discovered and nurtured. TV3 Mentor's nationwide reach highlighted its impact on shaping the music industry, providing a platform for budding artists to showcase their skills and embark on a life-changing musical journey. The show's influence extended far beyond the TV screens, leaving a lasting impact on the Ghanaian music scene.

Select participants from each audition center would be chosen to compete again in Accra for the grand audition, where the final twelve contestants would be selected for the live show. These contestants would then reside in the mentor house for the duration of the program. Each week, one or two contestants would be eliminated based on public votes and judges' scores, and would need to leave the mentor house.

At 3:30am on a Saturday, Mawu and Adjei set out from Adabraka to Kwame Nkrumah Circle, a distance of approximately 1.8km, to save money. They boarded a 37 bus and got off at the TV3 junction. Arriving at the TV3 premises at 4:35am, they found a small group of people already there for the audition. To avoid the long queue that would form later, Mawu arrived early, obtained her number card, and registered her name, securing the 20th position for the day's auditions. As more people arrived around 6:00am.

At 8:00am, the audition officially commenced, and the judges began assessing the talents of the contestants. When it was finally Mawu's turn, she took a deep breath, walked into the audition room, and delivered a captivating performance. Her powerful voice, impressive range, and emotional connection to the song left the judges in awe. After a brief moment of deliberation, the lead judge smiled and said, 'Mawu, your voice is truly exceptional. We'd like to see you again tomorrow for the final audition.' Mawu beamed with joy, feeling a mix of relief and excitement. She had made it to the next round! Adjei, who was waiting anxiously outside, was overjoyed when Mawu shared the news. Together, they left the premises, already looking forward to the final audition the next day.

The next day, Mawu and Adjei arrived at the TV3 premise at 6:00am sharp. They found other contestants already seated under a canopy on the premises and joined them, settling in to wait for their turn.

The atmosphere was electric, with some contestants rehearsing their songs and others strumming their guitars. Each performer was determined to give their best, knowing it was the final audition. With only twelve spots available in the live program, and 150 participants vying for them, the tension was palpable. Everyone was eager to secure a coveted spot among the final twelve contestants.

At exactly 8:30 am, the judges took their seats, marking the start of the audition. Mawu was the 18th contestant to be called. Adjei gave her his blessings and encouraged her to go in and showcase her talent. He remained outside, praying fervently for Mawu to be among the selected twelve. When Mawu's turn finally arrived, she took a deep breath and entered the audition room. A few minutes later, she emerged. "How did it go?" Adjei asked, his anxiety palpable..

"I gave it my all! Now it's just a waiting game. They won't announce the results until everyone's done auditioning. I'm getting pretty hungry, though. Want to come with me to grab some food?"

"I'm sure you'll make the cut! Let's just chill and wait for the results. I'm starving too, by the way"

They left the premises and enjoyed a delightful meal. Upon returning to the venue, they settled in with eager anticipation. The audition concluded at 4pm, and the producers meticulously tallied the results. A producer captured everyone's attention and began to announcing the names of the final twelve contestants. As the tension mounted, hearts raced with anxious anticipation. Eleven names were called, but Mawu's name had not been mentioned. Adjei's heart pounded incessantly, while Mawu's palms glistened with sweat. A palpable silence enveloped the space, with every heart pulsating, except for those eleven whose names had been announced. Finally, the producer declared, "Martha Music." Disappointment washed over those who hadn't heard their names. Mawu and Adjei departed for home, carrying a sense of disillusionment, yet maintaining a steadfast belief that this setback was not the end of their journey.

CHAPTER FOURTEEN

THE TURNING POINT

A month had passed since Mawu's mentor audition fell through, but she and Adjei remained undeterred. They continued their pursuit of opportunities, visiting top-notch 'A List' recording studios and presenting their proposals to beat engineers. However, they were met with disinterest, as these engineers showed little inclination to discover new talents, preferring to work with established artists instead. Undaunted, Mawu and Adjei recognized that true greatness requires perseverance and refused to be disheartened. Instead, they chose to redouble their efforts, more determined than ever to succeed.

Despite facing obstacles, Mawu and Adjei continued their market work while actively exploring ways to advance Mawu's career. As Christmas approached, the market became increasingly busy, with purchases and sales reaching a peak. The festive season always brought overcrowding to the market, but Mawu and Adjei saw an opportunity. They planned to work at Tudu market, a popular shopping destination during holidays, focusing on trading clothing, a high-demand commodity. They procured female dresses from a wholesale vendor and displayed them on their arms as they positioned themselves along Tudu's bustling streets to attract buyers. The season proved to be lucrative, allowing them to accumulate savings for the future. Recognizing the need to pave their own path to success, they remained dedicated in the absence of external interest in Mawu's artistic endeavors.

Amidst the festive atmosphere, shops were transformed with vibrant ribbons, flowers, and ornamental lights, enticing customers with discounts. Parents and children joyfully selected Christmas attire and footwear, adding to the lively scene. Among the throngs of shoppers, two young couples approached Mawu and Adjei, interested in their merchandise. Notably, a young boy followed the couples, skillfully capturing their interactions on an iPhone amidst the bustling marketplace, a feat that surprised Adjei, given the risk of pickpockets in the area. The couples purchase three female dresses, marking a successful transaction in the midst of the festive fervor.

"You two are absolutely stunning together! It's clear you're meant to be. Are you guys married?" Mawu smiled warmly and handed them their purchases in a polythene bag

"Not yet, but we're actually getting married next month in January!" The young gentleman replied with a smile, taking the package from Mawu.

"I'm so happy for you both! I wish you a lifetime of joy and happiness together," Mawu said with a warm smile, offering her blessings.

The gentleman and his fiancée thanked Mawu and flashed her a warm smile. Adjei, consumed by his insatiable curiosity, could not resist asking more question.

"So, why is this guy recording your every move? Are you guys celebrities or something?"

"No, we are not," the young man grinned.

"No worries, I'm just curious! Could this be some kind of pre-wedding video shoot?" Adjei asked with a grin.

"Honestly, I've been doing this video thing for a long time - even before I met my fiancée. I just love capturing life's moments and sharing them on social media. It's not about oversharing or seeking attention; I just find joy in documenting my journey. Whether I succeed or fail, every moment matters. From the highs to the lows, each experience makes our journey unique. That's why I think it's so important to record our lives and cherish every moment. Every experience is precious, so I want to preserve them for reflection later on," he said with a smile.

""Wow, this is amazing! Thanks for being so patient with my questions. I wish you both all the best, and be careful with that phone - there are some shady people out there who might try to take advantage of you," Adjei said with a concerned smile.

"Thank you, see you guys another time, Bye!"

A commotion erupted at the southern end of the market street, where a large crowd had gathered. A young woman in her thirties had been caught stealing three children - twin daughters aged 2 and a 3-year-old girl - from two vendors. The mothers, who were selling cotton lace fabric, had left their children seated in small plastic chairs beside them. However, their attention was diverted by the crowd of customers surrounding their merchandise. Seizing the opportunity, the young woman carried off all three children, securing the 3-year-old on her back and cradling the twins against her chest. Just as she was about to board a bus, a woman who knew the twins' mother approached her and inquired about the children's destination and their mother's whereabouts. When the young woman couldn't respond, the woman identified her as a thief and called for assistance. The twins' mother and the other woman, whose child had also been taken, arrived and were shocked to have not noticed their children being snatched. The young woman confessed to planning to sell the children to a woman who had been buying stolen kids from her for years. This woman would groomed the children and force them into prostitution at a young age. The young woman admitted to selling each child for 500 cedis.

The crowd almost pummeled her mercilessly, but the authorities intervened just in time and apprehended the young lady. Mawu and Adjei had already arrived at the scene and were observing the unfolding events.

"It's unbelievable that some women can be so heartless! As a woman herself, she knows the struggles of pregnancy and childbirth. I recall Mabel's story and the agony in her eyes. How could she do something so terrible, selling another woman's children for a mere 500 cedis? It's just appalling!" Adjei's indignation poured out as he spoke.

Mawu was shocked by the whole scene and was left speechless.

It was exactly 4:12pm on a prosperous late afternoon, and Mawu and Adjei had successfully concluded the sale of their garments. The new venture had proven to be highly lucrative, leaving them eager for more festive days like Christmas. They considered exploring another business opportunity or returning to their previous occupation of pushing trucks after the Christmas season. Despite the continued demand for clothing from numerous customers in the market, they decided to close up for the day due to a prior engagement. Their destination was the residence of Mr.

Larweh, a renowned music producer in Accra, located in Awoshie within the Ga Central Municipal Assembly. Adjei had obtained Mr. Larweh's contact information from an acquaintance and had arranged a meeting with him. Before heading to Awoshie, they decided to grab a bite to eat.

At precisely 5:30 pm, they arrived at Mr. Larweh's residence, where they were ushered to a shaded area in the courtyard. Shortly after, Mr. Larweh emerged, and they rose to greet him. After exchanging pleasantries, he asked them to sit. Mr. Larweh inquired about the purpose of their visit, and Adjei, taking the lead, explained that Mawu was a talented singer, songwriter, and composer seeking a manager to help her achieve her aspirations. He believed that Mr. Larweh, with his extensive experience and resources, was the ideal person to propel Mawu to stardom. Mr. Larweh nodded thoughtfully and turned to Mawu, asking what she could bring to the table if he agreed to manage her.

"I'm bringing something truly unique to the table. My compositions are like a fusion of the earth's rhythms and the human experience. I use my music as a way to comment on the world we live in, to highlight the absurdities and contradictions that make us human."

"Wait a minute, are you serious? You're coming at me with this over-the-top language, talking about your music like it's some kind of divine revelation? Please, spare me the drama," Mr. Larweh interrupted, his voice laced with sarcasm.

"Sir, may I please have the chance to fully express my ideas before you form an opinion? I'd be grateful if you could listen to me out," Mawu requested with courtesy and deference.

Enough! I'm talking, and you're interrupting. Don't you have any respect for your elders?" Mr. Larweh thundered, his voice rising in anger. "This meeting is over. Get out!" He stood up, his authority commanding attention, and ordered his security man, "Escort them out and lock the gate."

Mawu and Adjei were disheartened to discover that Mr. Larweh exuded an air of self-importance.

"I don't get it, what did I say wrong?" Mawu questioned, her voice laced with puzzlement and a hint of frustration.

"I believe he was intimidated by your confidence," Adjei replied with a knowing smile.

"I'm genuinely curious about this. Can you help me understand what true confidence looks like, and why it's often mistaken for arrogance? I want to make sure I'm not coming across the wrong way."

"In our African culture, speaking your mind or questioning the status quo can be seen as a sign of arrogance," Adjei observed.

"That's a great question - why should speaking up be seen as arrogant? Don't we have the right to question things, to suggest new ideas? Is our mindset so limited that we can't handle a little sophistication? Where did this misguided thinking even come from?".

"I've seen it time and time again in Ghana - our cultural norms seem to prioritize conformity over creativity. If you speak up or try to do things differently, you're often shut down and called arrogant. It's frustrating because I know we have so much talent and innovation to offer, but it's getting stifled by this mindset." Mawu observed.

The festive atmosphere of Christmas had dissipated, giving way to the harsh reality of January. Although January has the same number of days as December, it often feels interminably long to those who rely on monthly wages. The financial strain of holiday expenses leaves many eagerly awaiting the end of the month and their next paycheck. This financial burden is also felt in the market, where reduced consumer spending leads to sluggish sales.

On a tranquil Sunday morning, a day reserved for spiritual contemplation, relaxation, and preparation for the upcoming week, the warm sunlight and gentle silence created a sense of serenity The customary routine of daily labor was momentarily halted on Sundays, allowing for essential tasks such as laundry and upkeep of their surroundings to be completed. As Mawu and Adjei immersed themselves in their chores, their peaceful atmosphere was disrupted by the unforeseen arrival of Ansah, who appeared at their doorstep without a warning. Mawu, engrossed in conversation with Adjei, was caught off guard by Ansah's sudden presence, which left her feeling startled and uneasy A brief silence enveloped the trio as they exchanged inquisitive glances, leaving Adjei perplexed by the unspoken tension between Mawu and Ansah, which seemed to hang in the air like a challenge.

"Ansah! What are you doing here? How did you find me?" Mawu asked, her voice laced with surprise. "Who brought you here? Did someone tell you where I was? I'm pretty sure my parents have no idea I'm here"

"Whoa, slow down, Mawu! One question at a time, okay? Let me answer your last one: no, your parents have no idea you're here. I actually followed you last Monday when you were pushing a wheelbarrow around dusk. I've been keeping an eye on you since then."

"So, you two know each other or what?" Adjei asked, curiosity getting the better of him.

"Yeah! Ansah's a friend from back home. We grew up in the same neighborhood," Mawu explained.

. "Your sister asked about you, but I didn't know where you were at the time, so I told her I didn't know."

"And you still don't know, huh?" Mawu said with a hint of authority.

"Mawu, why did you leave your comfortable home? Is this really the life you want? You gave up your nice place for this tough neighborhood, and I just don't get it. When I saw you struggling last Monday, it broke my heart. I was so tempted to rush to your parents' house and tell your mom everything, but I wanted to talk to you first. So, please, help me understand why you left home and what's going on with you now."

"You know how I feel about my career goals, and you know my parents weren't on board with them. Honestly, I wasn't too thrilled about their expectations for me either. So, I left home to forge my own path and find some peace. My friend here has been a rock for me, a true brother and partner in every sense. We've been grinding and trying to make it happen, but it's tough. I know you recognize my talent, but I need guidance from someone who's already made it in the industry. Adjei and I are trying to do this on our own, but it's proving to be a real struggle."

"I can introduce you to Rolex, and I'm pretty sure he'll be willing to help you out."

"Who's Rolex?" Mawu asked, her interest piqued.

"Rolex was my senior in high school, and now he runs his own record label. I'll need to chat with him, but I'm sure he'll be able to help. I'll head out now and talk to him, and I'll come back tomorrow morning to fill you in on what he says. Or, do you have a number or something where I can reach you?"

"Sure thing, Ansah. Here's my number," Adjei said, rattling off his digits.

"Please, Ansah, keep my situation on the down low, okay? Don't mention it to anyone, not even your girlfriend. I'm begging you," Mawu said, her voice filled with concern.

Early the next morning, while they were working at the market, Adjei's phone rang,. It was Ansah, who instructed them to meet him at the Kwame Nkrumah circle so he could escort them to Rolex's place. They entrusted their wheelbarrow to Peter and hurried to meet Ansah.

When they arrived at Rolex's place, he welcomed them with open arms. His girlfriend, Lamisi, was there too, and she greeted them with a warm smile that made them feel at ease. Then, Rolex asked Mawu to show off her skills, and she blew him away with an amazing acapella performance and a medley of songs. He was so impressed that he offered her a record deal on the spot! He told her to come back in three days with her lawyer or manager to finalize the paperwork. Over the moon with excitement, they thanked him and said their goodbyes.

That night in the market, sleep was the last thing on their minds. Mawu and Adjei were bursting with joy, their hearts racing with excitement. The good news had electrified them, and they couldn't wait to leave their struggles behind. As they sat amidst the vibrant stalls, now empty and silent, they felt an overwhelming sense of hope and anticipation.

They gazed up at the starry sky, feeling the universe aligning in their favor. The hardships they had endured in the market, the countless nights spent under the open sky, the struggles to make ends meet – all of it seemed worth it now. They knew they were on the cusp of something incredible, something that would change their lives forever.

With every passing moment, their dreams seemed within reach. They could almost taste the sweetness of success, feel the thrill of achievement. And as they sat there, basking in the glow of their good fortune, they knew that nothing could stop them from reaching their destinies. The market, once a symbol of their struggles, had become a stepping stone to greatness.

With the paperwork and formalities finally out of the way, Mawu was now fully immersed in her dream career as a professional musician. She spent her days honing her craft, writing new songs, and rehearsing with her band. Meanwhile, Adjei had thrown himself into his new role as her dedicated personal manager, learning the ins and outs of the music industry and working tirelessly to promote Mawu's talent.

Their hard work and dedication had paid off in a big way. The record label had not only signed Mawu but also provided them with a comfortable apartment, a far cry from the humble kiosk they once called home in the bustling market. They now had a beautiful place to rest their heads, a space to create and inspire each other.

Thanks to Ansah's introduction to Rolex, the right person at the right time, their lives had taken a dramatic turn for the better. They were living their dream, and they knew it. Every day was a new opportunity to grow, to learn, and to make music that would touch the hearts of millions.

Mawu underwent comprehensive training in etiquette, wardrobe selection, and public speaking skills, honing her talents and preparing herself for the spotlight. Meanwhile, Rolex accompanied her to a prestigious recording studio for her inaugural professional recording session, a milestone moment in her burgeoning career. The session was a resounding triumph, captivating everyone present with Mawu's enchanting vocals and leaving a lasting impression on all who witnessed it.

Following the studio session, Rolex arranged for Mawu to have a photoshoot at a top-notch studio, where she was treated like a true star. The resulting photographs exuded elegance and sophistication, showcasing Mawu's innate star quality and hinting at the bright future that lay ahead. With her newfound skills, captivating voice, and stunning visual presence, Mawu was now ready to take the music industry by storm.

Ansah had been visiting Mawu to offer his expertise in social media management to her and the Rolly Empire. He was a successful public relations strategist for a reputable company. Living a comfortable life as a gentleman, Ansah's girlfriend, Lovely, was a talented fashion designer and costumier. However, Ansah had kept his visits to Mawu a secret from Lovely, as Mawu had specifically cautioned him to maintain confidentiality.

"So, what's new with your family? I've been seeing your sister Suzzy around a lot lately. She's living just a stone's throw away from me with her hubby. We've been saying hi and catching up a bit. How about you, when's the last time you spoke with them?"

"Honestly, I don't remember the last time I called home, but now that things are going well, I'll reach out soon. Wait, what? My sister's married? I had no idea! When did she tie the knot? I feel like I've been out of the loop for too long!"

"She was married and divorced before tying the knot again last June. And now, she's just had a baby!"

"So, Suzzy was married and then they split up, but what actually went wrong?" Mawu asked, settling comfortably into the plush sofa with a curious expression.

"Honestly, I'm not sure what happened, but that marriage almost destroyed your sister. I saw her a few times during that period, and I barely recognized her. She looked so frail and had lost her sparkle completely. I was relieved when I heard they'd finally divorced."

"Wow, that marriage must have been really tough for her to end it, because the Suzzy I know would never give up on her husband easily. And I know my parents would have been totally against the divorce too. But I'm just glad she's found happiness again. I need to reach out and congratulate her on the new baby soon!"

"By the way, how have you been? It feels like ages since you last stopped by - almost two months, right? What's new with you?"

"I'm doing great, thanks for asking! Work is going amazingly well too. And I'm thrilled to see your social media presence growing steadily every week. I'm really optimistic that when your new single drops, it'll be a game-changer. I think people will really connect with your music and want to learn more about you, which should lead to a big boost in followers across all your platforms. Fingers crossed!"

Four months later, Rolly Empire Records finished producing Mawu's music video and set a release date for her debut single. This moment marked the fulfillment of a long-held dream. After navigating a challenging and tumultuous path, she was now poised to embark on a smooth and successful journey in life.

The song's release was a resounding success, quickly gaining traction on the airwaves and marking a significant milestone in the music industry. As it hit various radio stations, its popularity skyrocketed, building momentum with each play. The infectious melody and heartfelt lyrics struck a chord with listeners, resonating deeply and generating a buzz that spread far and wide. With its captivating sound and relatable themes, the song drew audiences in, leaving a lasting impression and cementing its place in the music scene.

The catchy tune proved irresistible to listeners, who clamored for more, driving up airplay and sparking a surge in requests for repeat plays. The song's airwave dominance served as a testament to its broad appeal and profound emotional resonance, striking a chord with audiences far and wide. As its popularity continued to soar, artists and music aficionados took notice, hailing it as a standout track that was revolutionizing the industry.

CHAPTER FIFTEEN

THE ACCOMPLISHED MISSION

Mawu's soul-stirring ballad, "One Day," enthralled audiences with its melodic allure, resonating across diverse media platforms. The song's poignant lyrics, masterfully crafted by Mawu, painted a vivid tapestry of life's tribulations and triumphs, exploring themes of resilience, heartbreak, and ultimate victory.,Its universal appeal transcended boundaries, captivating even the Christian community, who found solace and inspiration in its redemptive message. Some pastors were so moved by the song's powerful narrative that they incorporated it into their sermons, recognizing its ability to touch hearts and minds. As "One Day" continued to echo through the airwaves, it became a beacon of hope, a testament to the music's enduring power to uplift and inspire in times of darkness.

As Mrs. Cynthia Johnson headed home after a long day's work, she turned on her car stereo, tuning into her favorite FM stations. To her delight, Mawu's song filled the airwaves, captivating her with its enchanting lyrics. The music brought her a sense of joy, but also stirred up a mix of emotions as her thoughts drifted to her daughter, Mawu, whom she hadn't seen in five years. The song's sweet melody and poignant words transported her back to memories of her daughter, and for a moment, she was lost in thought, nostalgia washing over her.

"I'll be back home once I've made my dream a reality," Mawu told her mom over the phone.

And so, five years had passed. As she pulled her car over to the side of the road, tears streamed down her cheeks. She took a moment to collect herself, allowing a single tear to escape. Her heart overflowed with hope at the prospect of reuniting with her daughter, but the question lingered – when would that day come? With a gentle swipe, she wiped away her tears, offering a fervent prayer to the divine to guide her daughter home.

Mawu was the toast of the entertainment industry, with her name on everyone's lips. Her concerts were always sold out, with fans clamoring to see her perform live. Her demand skyrocketed, with event organizers vying for her attention. She had become a household name among music enthusiasts, synonymous with talent and excellence. Television stations were eager to feature her, and she was frequently invited for interviews. One day, while Mr. Johnson was channel surfing, he stumbled upon a prominent TV station and was thrilled to see his daughter, Mawu, captivating the audience with her charm and wit in a live studio interview..

Today, we're celebrating women who embody professionalism, inner beauty, and virtue. And we're thrilled to introduce the incredible Miss Mawu, who's taken Ghanaian highlife music to new heights and won hearts globally. Her show-stopping performance at the recent BET Awards was a testament to her exceptional talent. But behind every success story lies a journey, and we're curious about the challenges she faced along the way. So, Mawu, can you share with us the obstacles you overcame and how you turned adversity into opportunity?" inquired the interviewer.

"Honestly, my parents weren't on board with my dreams. They wanted me to become a lawyer, but that just wasn't my passion. We butted heads, and I eventually left home to chase my aspirations. I found myself on the streets, alone and struggling, but I held onto hope. Luckily, I met Adjei, a loyal friend who took me under his wing and gave me a place to stay in the market. I faced some tough times - like a near-death experience in a market fire and a shady sound engineer who tried to take advantage of me. But I refused to give up. I persevered, and today, I'm proud of how far I've come," Mawu shared with a smile.

Mr. Johnson was captivated by the television screen, unable to tear his gaze away. The daughter he had once considered the black sheep of the family was now making a remarkable name for herself. The thought of people discovering that Mawu was his daughter filled him with a complex mix of emotions that defied description. Overwhelmed, he covered his face with his hands.

"I want to express my deepest gratitude to my amazing manager, Rolex, and his fiancée, Lamisi, my good friend Ansah, and Adjei, my trusted confidant. Thanks also to all my loyal supporters who've been with me every step of the way. I'll always be grateful to the streets, which embraced me when my own parents doubted me. The streets gave me solace and acceptance, and for that, I'll always have love and appreciation."

Mr. Johnson couldn't bear to watch the interview any longer; he switched off the television, unable to contain his emotions.

Mawu, Ansah, and Adjei were gathered at Mawu's residence, engaged in casual conversation, when her phone suddenly rang,. On the other end was Rolex, her esteemed manager, who conveyed the urgency of her presence at his residence at precisely 3:00 pm for the final rehearsal. In just three days, Mawu was scheduled to showcase her talents at a significant event: the 89th birthday celebration of the former president, expected to be attended by numerous dignitaries. This grand occasion presented a remarkable platform for Mawu to elevate her reputation globally. A vision she once shared with her late brother, Frank, whose unwavering support she deeply missed.

"So, when will you be heading home to see your parents?" Ansah inquired.

Mawu took a deep breath, exhaling softly as she smiled graciously. She then poured a glass of freshly squeezed juice, setting it on the table where they sat.

"I'll visit them after my performance, but first, let's concentrate on today's rehearsal. I have my last run-through this afternoon, so I want to make sure I'm fully prepared," Mawu explained.

"Please I am sorry," Ansah said.

"Sorry for what," Mawu asked, looking puzzled.

"Your sister is here to see you. She reached out to me earlier and I gave her the address. I'm sorry if it's an inconvenient time, but she was really keen to see you and wouldn't take no for an answer."

"It's fine, go ahead and let her in."

Ansah welcomed Suzzy at the entrance, and as she stepped inside, she was captivated by the grandeur of the house. The indoor swimming pool and spacious garage, housing three luxurious vehicles just ten meters away, left her in awe. Her gaze wandered, taking in the magnificence of her surroundings.

Mawu greeted Suzzy with a warm smile, which Suzzy reciprocated. They shared a tight embrace, tears glistening in their eyes, before pulling apart. Mawu then ushered Suzzy into the room, where they had a heartfelt conversation. Suzzy asked about Mawu's whereabouts during the intervening years, prompting Mawu to recount her arduous journey through the streets of Accra and her ventures in Dubai. Suzzy was moved to tears by her sister's struggles and experiences. In turn, Suzzy shared the story of her first marriage with Mawu. Observing Suzzy's radiant beauty, Mawu felt a sense of joy.

"I don't get it - you had my number, so why didn't you ever call or text me?" Suzzy asked.

"I actually sold my phone to fund a music project that didn't quite take off, so I lost my SIM card too. And to be honest, I was hesitant to reach out to you because I thought you'd tell Mom and Dad where I was, and I wasn't ready for that. Sorry, Suzzy," Mawu said with a gentle smile.

"So, when are you planning to see Mom and Dad? I already told Mom I was coming to visit you."

"I'll head over to their place within the next three days to visit them."

"You really should visit, Mom has been missing you so much and can't wait to see you."

"How is your husband doing?" Mawu asked.

"He is doing good. He is at home with Erica," Suzzy responded.

"Who is Erica?"

"My one-year-old daughter."

"I see! So you've given my English name to your daughter? That's sweet! I'll have to come by and meet her at home soon," Mawu said with a grin.

"Want to see a picture of her? Here she is!" Suzzy said, showing Mawu a photo on her phone.

"Wow, I'm happy for you."

Suzzy and Mawu dined together, after which Suzzy expressed her heartfelt gratitude to Adjei and Ansah for their unwavering support of Mawu. She then warmly embraced them before bidding them farewell and taking her leave.

The day of the former president's 89th birthday celebration had finally arrived, and the time was nearing for the event to commence. Several dignitaries had already arrived, and ushers were escorting them to their designated seats. Journalists mingled with distinguished guests, conducting conversations. Due to the high-profile nature of the event, security measures were exceptionally stringent. The audience included esteemed judges, lawyers, politicians, and musicians, all of whom had taken their seats. Suddenly, the piercing sound of a motorcade siren signaled the arrival of a six-vehicle convoy of Land Cruisers, which pulled up in the parking area. Ten security personnel disembarked from two of the vehicles - four wore sleek black suits, while those in police uniforms stationed themselves strategically outside the premises.

The former president emerged from his car with assistance and was escorted into the auditorium by the security detail in black suits, while those in police uniforms stationed themselves strategically outside the premises.

Inside the auditorium, an atmosphere of jubilation and excitement filled the air. The stage showcased live performances by talented musicians and comedians, captivating the audience's attention. Tables were elegantly set with a delectable array of food and beverages. As some attendees swayed and danced to the melodious tunes, others remained seated, tapping their feet, and nodding in harmony with the music. The former president's face radiated a warm smile, reflecting the joyous ambiance of the event. Following the previous performer's departure, the emcee gracefully took the stage to introduce the upcoming musician, seamlessly transitioning the evening's entertainment.

"Get ready for the musician everyone's been buzzing about! Her song has a powerful message that's resonated with so many people. You know her story - she's the young woman who dared to defy convention, leaving behind a life of luxury to chase her dreams on the tough streets with nothing but her determination. And she's killing it! Please welcome the incredible Ms. Mawu...!"

As Mawu ascended the stage, the audience applauded, the band began playing the instrumentals. Mawu started singing, and the auditorium fell silent, with the audience listening intently to the profound lyrics. Her music was lively and engaging, yet the words carried a depth that resonated with the audience's innermost being. Among the attendees were Mr. Johnson and Mrs. Johnson, whose eyes welled up with tears. Mr. Johnson delicately retrieved his handkerchief from his pocket to dab at his eyes, revealing the profound emotional impact the music had on him.

Mawu brought the house down with her performance, receiving a thunderous applause from the audience. The former president was so impressed that he beckoned her over, shaking her hand and then pulling her into a warm hug. The photographers snapped away, capturing the special moment from every angle. Mawu was over the moon with excitement, beaming with pride at the opportunity to meet the former president. After basking in the glow of her successful performance, she headed backstage and left for the outside with her crew. But her night wasn't over yet - waiting outside were journalists eager to ask her a flurry of question.

"We all saw that amazing hug with the former president! What was going through your mind in that instant?" inquired a journalist.

"I'm still on cloud nine after meeting the former president today! It was an absolute honor to shake his hand and share a warm hug. This moment is definitely one for the books - a real highlight of my life."

"You left behind a life of luxury to chase your dreams on the streets. What drove you to take such a huge risk? And what if things didn't work out - what if you ended up struggling to survive and your dreams remained just out of reach?" asked the journalist.

"You know those moments when you're outside in the early hours, around 2 or 3 am, and the morning dew starts to roll in? It's chilly, uncomfortable, and easy to get distracted. But I always remind myself that once the day gets going, the sun will shine bright. I don't waste time on negative thoughts or 'what ifs.' I'm a glass-half-full kind of person, always ready to tackle whatever comes my way. Yeah, life on the streets can be tough, but I never lost faith that I'd make it through. That mindset made everything else seem insignificant."

"There are assertions circulating that your biological parents are Mr. Ernest Johnson and Mrs. Cynthia Johnson. How accurate is this speculation?" inquired the journalist.

Ansah softly whispered some words into Mawu's ear. She turned around and saw her parents, their eyes brimming with tears. Rushing towards them, she embraced them tightly. Her mother tenderly kissed her forehead, while her father, his expression revealing deep remorse, gazed at her in silence.

"Daddy, I told you I will make it," Mawu grinned.

Mr. Johnson was rendered speechless, his only response being a cascade of tears.

"Will you still look down on me as a musician?" Mawu asked, her voice laced with sadness..

"I don't feel that way anymore. I've realized that musicians like you have an incredible gift - you can bring people together and touch hearts with your music. And tonight, you've shown me just how powerful that is. Your music is a source of comfort for so many, and that's a truly special thing. And as for me, my love for you, my dear daughter, knows no limits."

Acknowledgement

It would be very ungrateful on my part if this book is accomplished without stamping my profound gratitude to Dr. Shrikrishna Singh for his guidance, inspiration, and squeezing water out of stone in the dry season and leaving no stone unturned in helping me accomplish my diploma and first degree in Journalism with honors successfully. A sincere THANK YOU for recognizing my academic talents and passion to succeed.

I consider myself fortunate to have excellent teachers, especially Mr. Jackson Asante, and Christiana Kyei, at Multimedia Institute of Ghana who inspired me to continue my talent as a writer and further my academic career in Master's Program at the University of Ghana.

My sincere thanks to Oheneba Nana Safo Kantanka for his genuine support and sincere advice in every aspect of the journey to accomplish and overcome challenges, if any.

My heart felt "thanks" to Jennifer Asare and Gloria Arthur for their friendly suggestions and keeping me cheerful during cloudy days.

To the Auctus publishers team, I thank everyone for their various roles they played to make this book a success.